ALIEN THRILL SEEKER

ALIEN THRILL SEEKER

ADRENALINE RUSH™ BOOK TWO

LAWRENCE M. SCHOEN
BRIAN THORNE

LMBPN
DISRUPTIVE IMAGINATION®

LMBPN Publishing
PMB 196, 2540 South Maryland Pkwy
Las Vegas, NV 89109

Version 2.00, August 2022
ebook ISBN: 979-8-88541-744-0
Print ISBN: 979-8-88541-745-7

THE ALIEN THRILL SEEKER TEAM

Thanks to our Beta Team

Kelly O'Donnell

Thanks to our JIT Readers

Wendy L Bonell
Zacc Pelter
Deb Mader
Dave Hicks
Jeff Goode
Peter Manis
Diane L. Smith

If We've missed anyone, please let us know!

Editor
The Skyfyre Editing Team

DEDICATION

This volume is dedicated to our dogs,
past and present, who have made our lives fuller by their simple presence and companionship.
Life is just better with dogs.

And no, Potato is not even close to being a dog,
but please don't tell Coop.

CHAPTER ONE

Ben Cooper's head pounded. His brain housing unit throbbed, and his mouth tasted like ass. He knew the signs all too well, having learned them over the course of more than forty years of overindulgence and resulting hangovers. Later, he'd hydrate and that would help, but for now the trick was to avoid actually waking up. He kept his eyes squeezed tightly shut and rolled to his right with every intention of returning to sleep.

That's when he bumped into the body.

Coop's eyes shot open, all thought of his aching head or the healing power of sleep having vanished. Light flooded his retinas. He groaned in discomfort and blinked rapidly. When his eyes adjusted, he tried to make sense of what he saw, hoping it might trigger his memory of how he'd gotten there.

The body belonged to a young woman, and while it wasn't a new experience for the aged actor to wake up hungover and in bed with a lovely companion, it was the first time he could recall doing so fully clothed.

Seconds ticked by as Coop stared at the twenty-something woman's face. He frowned. Twenty-something might be generous. Too young. Despite being in his sixties, Coop's big-screen charisma had never waned and he routinely bedded women decades his junior, but this was a bit extreme. This woman hadn't even been alive back when his career had peaked. The presence of his clothing suggested he hadn't done anything inappropriate and his expression transitioned from frown to smile. He'd never had a problem waking up with ladies he had little personal familiarity with. Confirmation that women still had trouble resisting his charms stroked his ego. Still, he was pretty sure it was the first time he'd woken up next to a woman in a coma. A pretty, dark-haired woman in a coma.

That should mean something.

And then his brain kicked in and provided the missing piece.

Coma. Shit! It's Tycho!

Memories flooded Coop's mind. The Box aliens—stupid, arrogant, smarmy robot-inhabiting aliens—and their bullshit medical experiments. And his escape from their demented custody with Tycho—the comatose young woman in bed with him—and Dr. Jessica Acorns, the pretty young researcher who had helped him escape the Box ranch and almost certain death. Jess liked Coop, even if she didn't know it yet. In fact, the last thing he remembered was driving...er, crashing one of the Box's vehicles over the wall of their compound. After that, he had *nada*.

Coop pushed himself up on the bed and looked around.

The room was...less than stellar. In his glory days, he'd enjoyed some pretty posh accommodations, and while those times were well behind him, they provided a benchmark. This room wasn't even up to the reduced standards he held for himself. Nor even up to the standards he'd tolerated when his agent and manager reminded him he was broke. This room just plain sucked.

It wasn't just small—it was oppressively small. Cramped even. Purple wallpaper with a metallic gray *fleur-de-lis* motif covered the walls and gave the room a nineteenth-century feel at odds with the modern fluorescent ceiling. Not that there was much worth illuminating. A large bed took up most of the space. The mattress felt like little more than a metal shelf with a worn-out layer of packing peanuts, wrapped up in dingy sheets that smelled like old sex and potpourri. *Eww.* Taking in the rest of the room revealed a dim mirror mounted on a side wall, a small door that led to what Coop presumed would be an equally disappointing bathroom, a dinky bedside table that projected the time onto its adjacent purple wall, and a solitary chair currently occupied by an annoyed looking Dr. Jessica Acorns.

Annoyed. But still pretty.

Coop immediately adjusted his posture to project a more confident mien to the young woman. It was a reflex. He couldn't help it. He was Ben "Coop" Cooper, action star. People expected and received a certain level of casual confidence from him regardless of what was happening around him. Forty years in the business had taken their toll, and sometimes—like now—his learned habits of projecting the right image replaced his ability to act like a normal human being. He could play one with ease. He just couldn't always remember to *be* one.

"About time you woke up," Jess grumbled.

Coop turned his head to the right. Jess' tone told him he was in trouble, but since he didn't know why, he instinctively opted to give her his best side. His headshot side. The side with the tiny scar from a fall off a playground jungle gym when he was a toddler. He always said it was from a bar fight, but it wasn't. Having the correct backstory was important, as were all the tiny details that fed it. That bit of a scar provided a little something extra that gave women pause and ultimately made them swoon. Not that the right side of his face was anything to scoff at, mind you.

He needed a minute to think. And he needed information.

"Where are we?" he finally asked.

"The Four Seasons, of course. Did you sleep well? Would you

like room service? A pot of tea perhaps? What do you mean, 'where are we'? This hellhole was your idea."

Coop shook his head. That did not make sense. He'd never choose a room like this—better to sleep in a park. Ben Cooper did not stay in dingy places on purpose.

"Why does it look like a cheap French whorehouse?"

Jess raised an eyebrow at him with incredulity. "Because it is a whorehouse, Mr. Cooper. And yes, surely a cheap one. Not that I have any basis for comparison myself. Why do you keep asking stupid questions? You were the one who robbed the bank machine. You were the one who came up with the idea to hide out in a brothel. More, you were *insistent* about it. This was all you, Mr. Cooper. So please stop asking me to explain it."

Coop blinked again. *I did what?*

"Jess, I have no clue what you're talking about. The last thing I remember is crashing over the wall back at the ranch..."

The back of Coop's head, near the base of his skull, began to itch.

«A bordello is a classic hiding place, Ben. It's been used by all the greats in some of the most important movies ever made. Heck, you can't make a western without a good brothel. It would be a sin.»

Despite years of habit and a reputation for one of the best poker faces on any movie set, the color drained from Coop's expression. *The voice!* Coop remembered the voice in his head. It had appeared seconds before he'd lost control of his body and caused their escape vehicle to pop up on two wheels and scale the Box compound's wall in near-suicidal fashion.

«Ben, are you listening?»

Yes. But why? Who are you?

«No time for all that, buddy. Just pay attention. The Box are going to be after us. We're still in serious trouble.»

Super.

«Fortunately for you and the lovely and talented Dr. Acorns over there, I knew that. Just like I knew a brothel would be the ideal place for

a guy to hide out with two attractive young women. Especially when one of them is comatose. And did I mention Dr. Acorns? Man, brains are so attractive.»

Do I want to know why you have experience with these things?

«Don't worry about it, Ben. Time is of the essence.»

Who are you and why are you in my head?

«Am I so easily forgotten? You really don't pay attention. I'm Dyrk.»

Coop suddenly remembered. The voice had told him his name before he'd blacked out.

"Mr. Cooper? Hello? Are you with me?"

He shook his head and focused on Jess. She had a concerned look on her face.

"Sorry, Jess. What?"

"You looked like you went somewhere else. Your eyes were glazed over. Are you feeling okay?"

Coop was most certainly not feeling okay. He was on a moon in Saturn's orbit, running from psychotic aliens, infected with an immortal virus, and now he was either possessed or losing his damn mind.

"No. No, Jess. I'm not okay." He took a deep breath and steadied himself. If anyone could help him right now, it was her. He just wasn't very good at admitting he needed help. Especially not to young women. "I really don't remember anything after we got out of the compound. And now there's a voice in my head. Don't give me that look. I'm telling you what's happening to me. The voice, he calls himself Dyrk. And it isn't the first time I've heard him. He spoke to me right before I drove us over the wall at the Box compound. Or maybe he drove us over. I'm pretty sure I lost control of my body right around then. I must have blacked out after that and just woke up here."

Jess gave him a strange look. "No, you didn't. You've been conscious the whole time. First you drove us into the city at warp speed in a damaged transport. Then you hacked that bank machine and grabbed all the credits before dragging us halfway around the spaceport, where you abandoned our vehicle at a public entrance. You paused only long enough to strap Tycho to her gurney so you could push her pell-mell through back streets and alleys until we reached some seedy area behind a bunch of dive bars. You started asking around for a whorehouse, and when we got here you handed over most of the stolen money to the alien madam running this nightmare establishment."

"You think I did that? Seriously? That doesn't even sound like me."

Jess ignored him and went on. "You tossed Tycho over your shoulder, climbed the stairs to the *Ambassadorial Room,* popped her down on the bed, and immediately collapsed alongside her." She finished with a mocking sweep of her arms.

"I don't remember any of that."

"Really? Because it certainly seemed like you'd done this before. I'm guessing theft and whorehouses aren't new territory for you."

"First off, I've never been to a whorehouse."

Jess looked at him skeptically.

"I'm a star, Jess. Stars don't need to go to prostitutes. If we want for company, there's an endless line of young lovelies hoping to spend time with us. Why are we talking about this? At any rate... I've never been anywhere like this and I sure as hell don't know a damn thing about hacking a bank machine. Nothing you said makes any sense. It just isn't possible. Now, if you'd said I'd charmed someone into helping us, sure. That I could believe."

Jess rested her face in the palms of her hands and groaned.

That isn't a helpful response.

"Jess, I swear. I don't remember anything after the stunt-driving back at the ranch."

«*That's because I handled all of that,*» Dyrk chimed in. «*And now that we're safe for the moment, we need to discuss our plans.*»

"Uh, Jess. Dyrk says he did the driving, and now we need to discuss our plans."

The young doctor lifted her head just enough for her pretty eyes to meet Coop's. "Oh, he does? Sure, why not."

Coop wasn't wholly convinced that Jess believed him. *Oh, well.*

«All right, Ben. Here's the deal. The next commercial vessel doesn't leave for Earth for a week. And believe me, the tickets will not be cheap. We're going to need three of them. Plus fake IDs for everyone. That means we need to lay low and hide out from the Box while we procure what we need to get off this rock. All of this is going to require more cash, and we can't risk the money machine thing again, not that it would have the kind of funds we need anyway. You with me so far?»

Sure. That makes sense.

«Good. And one more thing. We have to go back to the ranch and rescue Potato.»

Coop choked out loud. *You've lost your damn mind, Dyrk. Is it your mind? Have you lost* my *mind? This is too confusing.*

«No time for all that, Ben. Now tell Jessica what I just told you.»

Coop considered arguing but decided that would just be crazy. Or *crazier,* at any rate. So, he dutifully relayed Dyrk's plans to Jessica, who buried her face back in her hands and muttered, "This is not happening. You have got to be kidding me."

"I wish I was, Jess. But he seems pretty determined."

"Mr. Cooper, did you forget what the Box want to do with you? You know, the vivisection? Cutting you open while you're alive to see how the virus works. Do you remember that?"

A chill of fear raced down Coop's spine. He *had* forgotten that part. *Oh, hell no.*

The base of his skull began to itch and throb. In the next instant, Dyrk's presence somehow jumped to the front of Coop's consciousness, taking control of his body and speaking to Jessica using Coop's mouth.

«Let me spell it out for you, Doctor. Scatola is many things, but he isn't a fool. There's a remote possibility that he hasn't figured out that your efforts with the virus have worked, maybe not to what extent, but unless you scrubbed the facility's surveillance footage, we have to assume he knows by now.»

Jess lifted her head up. "Surveillance footage?"

«The Box document *everything*. You know this.»

"Well, yes, but—"

«Do you have any reason to doubt they have a gazillion cameras, all hooked up to timers or motion sensors, running in every room and corridor? Do you think a race of über-wealthy anal-retentive AI-beings with a passion for knowledge-capture and a hardwired need to treat everything like an algorithm would have left anything to chance when it comes to documentation?»

"I don't... Wait, how do you even know about such things, Mr. Cooper?"

Dyrk sighed. «Coop knows about being *on* camera. I know about security, which is the matter at hand. Now, back on track. Once the Box are convinced that your research has borne fruit, they will try again. They might well screw it up, but as long as they have Potato, they will continue to make systematic attempts until either they succeed or Potato dies. And as you know, Potato can't die, which means he will suffer an eternity of torture alongside whatever new guinea pigs the Box procure.»

Jessica nodded slowly, following the logic if not totally convinced about the whole Dyrk thing. "Why are you telling me this?"

«Because it informs our next course of action. We must rescue Potato from the Box.»

"Rescue him? Why?"

Inside his own head, Coop shouted, *Yeah, why? Let's just get the hell out of Dodge!*

«I would think your Hippocratic oath would make that clear, Dr. Acorns. The damage the Box will do to other humans—healthy individuals, not just the terminal patients you worked with—in pursuit of recreating an effective version of the virus, that's ultimately all on your head. But even if that doesn't motivate you, there's a much more basic reason why we need to save Potato.»

"What's that?"

«He's my family. Kin. He's blood.»

"Kin? You're some kind of self-aware hallucination living in an old man's head. How is a non-sapient furry alien animal related to you?"

Old man? That was unnecessary.

«That should be obvious to you, Doctor, given that you helped bring me into being. I'm not a hallucination. I'm very real. I'm a persona created by a portion of the virus that you shaped by exposing Potato to thousands of hours of videos and then passed on to Ben Cooper. That transfer gave me access to a functional mind and allowed me to achieve consciousness.»

"So this…entity I'm talking to, it's the virus?"

Dyrk smiled with Coop's face. «In part. You understand, I'm not one hundred percent sure, but I'm the result of the virus having melded with this body. The virus that lives in Potato is like me, but it's asleep, held back by the organism it inhabits.»

Jessica shook her head again. "That doesn't make any sense. Potato isn't the virus. He's the host for the virus."

«Good catch. But it's more complicated than that. You see, Potato and the virus are symbiotic. One can't live without the other. In fact, Potato was the catalyst for my awakening. If its pheromones hadn't come in contact with Ben, my own mutagenesis would not have begun. It's a one-time event, like with your human chicken pox, but it's what granted me access to Ben's frontal lobe and other cognitive regions. That's what enabled my evolution to a fully realized persona. A.k.a. Dyrk, at your service.» He sketched a short bow.

Jessica sat up straight and drummed her fingers against her lips. "Okay, Dyrk. I hear you, but it still doesn't make sense. All of my research suggests that the virus feeds on adrenaline. This explains why it only seems to activate when there is some kind of stressor, a fear stimulus, which allows it to heal during fight-or-flight situations."

«Correct. Go on, Doctor.»

"But I've studied Potato. Extensively. And it doesn't have adrenal glands. Its nervous system doesn't utilize and can't produce adrenaline."

«Right,» agreed Dyrk. «Do you think that's an accident? Ask yourself: if you created a sapient virus that could heal any injury and provided veritable immortality, would you leave it in a vessel that organically and uncontrollably produces the one thing it needs to activate itself? That wouldn't be very smart. While the Box may be a glorious collection of jackasses, their creators—whoever they were—clearly were not stupid.»

Jessica stood and paced the length of the room. Due to its ridiculous size, she could only move six steps in each direction. "This is too much. There is no way we can get Potato out of their clutches. The Box will kill us. They'll have their ranch locked up tight. You can say whatever you want, but I didn't sign on for this and I am *not* responsible for it."

Dyrk gave her a cold stare. «I understand it's human nature to avoid accountability, and I don't blame you for that. But if you're not responsible, who do you imagine is?»

The conversation dragged on, a boring mixture of the philosophical and the clinical. Coop did his best to follow along but failed miserably until, with no warning, he felt himself flow back toward the front of his mind. It was a sensation akin to sliding down a Jell-O–filled water slide, and when he hit bottom he was in control of his body once more.

Coop flexed his fingers. "Ah, that's better."

"What is?" Jessica asked, clearly perplexed.

"I'm back."

"Mr. Cooper? Does this mean Dyrk's gone? Because this is way past the point of getting weird."

"I'm not sure he's actually gone. It's kind of hard to explain. But he's not in the driver's seat right now, if that makes sense."

Jessica resumed pacing.

"So, Jess. Honey..."

"Yep, it's you."

Coop shrugged. "I get that all this *sciencey* stuff is fascinating for you and Dyrk. But like he said, we've got some pretty immediate problems to deal with, and a week at most to do them. Scatola and his douchey Box friends are out there. Who knows what kind of resources they can bring to bear to find us? We need to focus and figure out how we're going to get off this rock. And we need to start doing it right now."

«*Now you've got it.*» Dyrk's voice was sonorant and captivating in Coop's mind. «*And don't forget, we've got to save Potato. That's nonnegotiable. I'm not going anywhere without him, and neither are you.*»

Coop felt a chill race down his spine as Dyrk's threat hit home, then the virus slipped through and relegated Coop to the cognitive peanut gallery inside his own head. Dyrk turned to Dr. Acorns. «I've just informed Cooper that I'm not leaving Titan without Potato. I can't. It's not in my nature to. You understand that, right, Doctor?»

Jessica stopped pacing. "What? Dyrk? This is getting ridiculous. We need a cowbell to announce your comings and goings. Or something. And why on Earth, or Titan, would I understand anything that motivates you?"

«We've been through this. You shaped me. You molded the primordial clay of my being like a tiny feminine Zeus. I have the personality that I have because of you. You, Dr. Acorns, are the manipulative god of my origin story.»

"Whoa. No. Just... no. Don't blame me for this mess. If I could design a man's personality, I promise this wouldn't be it. Ask any woman. Ever. Besides, I've got enough to deal with, so I'm not adding you to my list."

«Fair enough. But to be clear, the films you showed Potato before you drew the virus from it are the building blocks of my persona. Thousands of hours of adventure and impossible missions. Espionage, weapons, and cunning. Explosions and car chases. I'm the amalgam of all that testosterone and badassery. That's a word, right? Anyway... Even if I wanted to do otherwise —which I most certainly do not—I'm constitutionally incapable of leaving an asset like Potato behind.»

"You're saying...you're an action hero?"

Dyrk caught her gaze, and damned if his eyes didn't gleam in the dim light of the bordello bedroom. He smoldered like the Rock in *Jumanji* and he knew it. «Yes, Doctor. I'm that and much more. I'm also a clandestine intelligence operative and master of covert...stuff! The time is coming when we'll need action, but right now we need planning. I have an idea on how to save Potato, but it's going to take time to set up. First, we're going to need—»

KNOCK, KNOCK, KNOCK.

Dyrk and Jessica turned toward the door.

The knocks repeated more insistently. With a suspicious glance at Dyrk, Jessica opened the door. The bordello's proprietress waddled in on two pairs of legs.

The madam, Zana, was a Cormyrian, a four-legged humanoid from somewhere in the galaxy, far, far away. She was like the reptilian version of a centaur. Her skin was purple and lightly scaled, but her face was pretty even by human standards, with an elaborately carved, expensive-looking obsidian ring shoved through her septum. Her hair hung like a wave of silver silk down her back, continued along the ridge of her spine, and culminated in a tail at her rear. Her only clothing was a black leather utility sash, snug against her flat chest.

As she shoved her way into the already cramped confines of

the room, Zana pulled a tablet from her sash and thrust it at the humans.

"You two need to see this." Her voice was breathy as she gestured with the electronic device until Coop accepted it.

Jess peered over his shoulders, and they watched as a video played. A logo marked the recording as originating with the Titanian News Service. It began with a male newscaster in a studio speaking to a colleague at a remote location. The image shifted to a makeshift podium in front of one of the spaceport's vehicular airlocks. A press conference was being given by one of the iterations of Scatola, the erudite but insufferable Box that had employed Dr. Acorns and recruited Ben Cooper. They watched with growing dread as the Scatola extension informed representatives of the Titanian government that the Box ranch had been compromised by "thieves and terrorists," and that invaluable medical research had been stolen. If the situation was not made right within the next forty-eight hours, the Box collective would have no choice but to void their lease, implode their habitats, and remove all Box presence and funding from the moon of Titan. From the reactions of the governmental reps, Scatola's threat was not what they'd expected. The image cut back to the news anchor, who blathered and recited facts about the significant and essential economic contributions provided by the Box. With a promise for more updates as they occurred, the broadcast cut to a commercial.

Dr. Acorns looked up at Zana with a clear attempt to appear both ignorant and innocent written across her face. "Why did you bring this to us?"

Zana gazed down her nose at Jessica and snorted in humor. "Little human, you don't run a successful business like mine without learning how to read people. Or by being stupid." She paused and gestured to Tycho laid out on the bed in just her hospital gown. "Not to mention, you brought that young lady in on a medical gurney before your man here threw her over his shoulder and carried her up here to the honeymoon suite," she finished sarcastically.

"I can explain that—" Jessica began, but the madam cut her off.

"Please don't. It's not my concern, nor is it even close to the creepiest or most disturbing stuff I've witnessed in my day. Humans are...complicated. Your complications provide me with a nice living, so I don't judge. Now, while it's no business of mine, dear, when I saw that Box talk of theft and medical research, and I recalled the circumstances of your arrival, well... I thought you'd want to know about the news."

The doctor's expression of feigned innocence transformed to light panic. "You won't tell anyone, will you?"

The madam snorted. "I keep much worse secrets than this every single day. Call it a professional courtesy. Speaking of which, what *is* your plan? You do have a plan, don't you?"

«We haven't gotten that far. Obviously, we want to get back to Earth. As soon as it is possible.»

Jessica bit her lip. "That newscast will have made departure harder than ever."

Zana nodded her understanding. "Maybe I can help. There is a bar in the Warrens called Hugo's. I have an associate... Someone with a history of extracting people. He sometimes works out of that bar. You may be able to negotiate the help you need from him. I'll send him a message."

"How do we recognize him?"

"You won't. He'll recognize you. It will be up to him to decide whether or not he chooses to do business with you."

The madam left the tablet in Coop's hands. She turned to depart, which forced the humans to back against the wall until she had left the room.

«This is a disaster,» Dyrk groaned, still in control of Coop's body.

"Really? *Now* you see this as a disaster. Because things were going so swimmingly before?"

«I'm not worried about the Box hunting us down like fugitives to catch or kill us.»

"You're not? That's comforting."

«Not at all. While that might lead to horrific mutilation and perhaps unending medical experimentation, that's all stuff I can handle. No, I'm concerned that the Box are talking about leaving Titan. I can't let that happen, not if we're to rescue Potato. They've just altered our timetable. We're now down to forty-eight hours. Maybe even less.»

As he finished speaking, Dyrk staggered and stumbled against the wall. He caught himself with one hand and avoided sliding down to the floor.

«Sorry about this. Maintaining control and... talking... it's exhausting. How do you humans do this all the time? I think I need to recede and consider our options. But don't worry, Dr. Acorns, I promise you I'll be back.»

Somehow, Jessica managed to roll her eyes and look concerned at the same time.

Dyrk responded with a curt nod, and in the next instant his entire posture changed. He no longer needed to support himself on the wall. He also seemed less...intense.

Coop slumped down and sat on the bed.

"What the hell did he mean by 'recede'? What's happening to me, Jess?"

"I don't know. And I hate not knowing stuff."

He stared at her in wide-eyed amazement. "That's not the answer I was looking for. How can you not know? Isn't this your virus? It's in my head. It picks fights with people who should have been my drinking buddies. It punches cops and flirts with young women. Wait. I'm guilty of that last one too, and it's not so bad. But your virus makes me jump off buildings, for God's sake!"

"Don't overreact, Mr. Cooper."

"Overreact? Jess, with the exception of my liver, I have a very well-developed sense of self-preservation, and it's clear that Dyrk does not share it. Your virus has given me a new lease on life, and I'd like to experience some of it. That's not overreacting. It's just survival."

Jess' mouth opened but no sound came out. Coop continued to stare. She swallowed and tried again.

"Mr. Cooper, let's calm down and approach this logically. Could you hear yourself when he was speaking through you?"

"Yes. It was like watching a movie through the camera."

"Okay. Well, let's try to put it in cinematic terms. He's the paradigm of an action hero. You're an actor. You should understand what that means."

"You're not getting it. Those are *characters*, Jess! Not people. It's fake. What you're describing is the *fictional* end result you see on the screen, not the actor portraying the role. There's no person behind it. Maybe a bit of backstory that provides some of the character's motivation, but no real experience."

Jess frowned. It made her look older, and an older Jess was exactly what Coop needed at that moment. Older, wiser, something like that, though she was still crazy attractive. Less hot would help him concentrate. Later, if they all survived, there'd be time to flirt and see where things might go.

"So... you're saying this Dyrk isn't real?"

Cooper remembered the exhilaration from dozens of films where he'd inhabited the role of an action hero, kicking ass and taking names. "Oh, he's real, all right. He's just fucking clueless, and I'm afraid he's going to get us all killed."

CHAPTER TWO

Coop watched as Jess resumed her pacing. She opened the door to the small bathroom, adding two extra steps each way by walking into the lavatory before turning around. He'd finally gotten through to her, and pacing was her way of processing it all. Judging by the stress written across her face, it wasn't helping much.

"This is crazy, Mr. Cooper. There is no way we can pull this off. We don't even know how many iterations of the Box exist. There could be countless Box-inhabited robots marching around with nothing better to do than hunt us. We don't even know how many worlds they occupy. They've been out in space a lot longer than us. If that wasn't bad enough, they possess technology far more advanced than we do, things you've never imagined. Not to mention an almost limitless supply of monetary resources. They never tire or need sleep. How are we supposed to get Potato away from them and escape? And even if we could manage to abscond with Potato and get off Titan, they'd still come after us. They are relentless. It's their nature. They don't understand the idea of giving up. Oh, we're so screwed!" Hearing her own words, Jess clamped both hands over her mouth, like that could help. She kept pacing.

Coop didn't have any answers, and Jess' panicked commentary just fueled his own agitation. He started to pace too. The two of them fell into a routine where they passed each other next to the bed as they wore a virtual rut in the bordello's floor.

They'd been at it for several minutes of tense silence and pointless motion when Jessica found her voice again. "What are we going to do, Mr. Cooper? It's not just me, right? This is all incredibly hopeless."

Coop continued his own tiny circuit of the bedroom's limited confines. Once, twice, and a third time before he stopped in the middle of the room and blocked Jess' path.

"I wasn't always a film actor," he informed her. "I actually began on the stage, doing summer stock and some really bad off-off-off Broadway productions. *Really* bad." He shivered at the memory. "This one time—I was no older than Tycho there—I had a supporting role in a remake of *Much Ado About Nothing,* and half the cast came down with food poisoning and couldn't perform. It was the second night of the show and we had a full house. The theater has that saying about how the show must go on. Which sounds great, in theory, but it's hard when everyone's either puking or crapping and sometimes doing them simultaneously. Yuck."

Jess wrinkled her nose at the imagery. "So, what happened?"

"We made do. Every actor doubled up on roles. Some of the parts were performed using puppets that the property manager found in storage. Lesser roles were edited out of scenes half an hour before curtain, their critical lines doled out to other characters."

«*You're saying you improvised,*» Dyrk's voice echoed in Coop's head. «*Improvise. Overcome. Adapt. These are the things action heroes do best! Just like Clint Eastwood in* Heartbreak Ridge. *Or MacGyver. Remember him? That guy was a badass.*»

"Shut up and let me think!"

"I'm sorry." Jess looked wounded.

"No. Not you, Jess. Dyrk. Well, both of you. Please just let me think for a minute."

Coop wasn't a terribly introspective guy. A lifetime of doing whatever the hell he pleased had taught him that introspection almost always ruined fun. He'd kicked the habit decades ago, shortly after he'd tanked his career by doing the right thing. Even so, on occasion he was capable of dusting off his moral compass and trying to get his bearings. Rare occasions, but they happened.

The problem was, Coop didn't know what he wanted, let alone what might actually be the right thing to do. He'd spent his entire existence worrying about one person: Ben Cooper. And that was a handful. Now, at the end of a long and self-indulgent life, he suddenly found himself not only responsible for his own screwed-up situation, but for the safety of Jess too. And even Potato, for that matter. To be fair, Potato was really cute. But what chance did Coop have of saving him?

Sure, he felt better than he'd felt in twenty years. He even looked better, which wasn't easy to achieve—Ben Cooper was no slouch in the looks department. It was like he'd been reborn, given a second chance by some benevolent god who looked after drunks and really, really handsome men. That was a god Coop could respect.

He stopped pacing and smiled at himself in the mirror.

Did he have the ability to pull this off? He had Dyrk, who apparently had some serious ninja skills. But Dyrk was only one man... Well, actually, he wasn't even that. More like an echo made up of endless characters from action films. Except...that echo had proved capable of taking over and running around in Coop's body. That was an important fact and probably a solid mark in the positive column. But on the negative side, they would be going up against what amounted to a fortified compound full of alien robots with no respect for human life.

Yeah. That's definitely a negative. But don't I owe Dyrk for saving me? Do I owe Potato?

The voice in his head remained silent, which suited Coop fine.

He didn't like owing debts, either monetary or personal obligations. He'd spent the last decade spiraling into an ever-deepening financial hole and constantly calling in favors from the handful of colleagues who'd still answer their phones when they saw it was him. It had sucked. He had never been able to get ahead of it and eventually had just stopped trying. Now, this new responsibility had to be the biggest debt he'd ever owed. After all, Jess had treated him with the virus that produced Dyrk, and Dyrk had healed him. The doctors on Earth had insisted he'd be dead from cirrhosis in six months. In the past several days, Jess' virus had cured his liver and removed the scourge of alcoholism. That stupid echo in his head had saved Coop's life. Period. No debate. End of discussion.

But should I throw away that gift on a suicide mission? That would be a total waste of it. And yet... What about Potato's life? Man, morality is really complicated. And no fun.

Potato. The Box had poked and prodded the poor alien animal for centuries. Sure, it was a dumb creature. Really, really dumb. But that didn't mean it deserved to be experimented on or held prisoner. It was...wrong.

Wasn't I ready to throw it all away a few days ago? To free Potato from their sadistic grasp? Yes. Yes, I was. That was very heroic of me. No surprise, of course. But still, quite admirable.

Coop didn't dwell too much on the chemical and biological effects that had been in play when he'd decided to take Potato out into Titan's toxic atmosphere with him. He knew what Jess thought: that his near-suicidal actions had been brought on by some combination of null-space syndrome, the virus in his blood, and Potato's pheromones. But deep down, Coop knew he had been heroic. It didn't matter that no one else understood that.

Yeah. That was me. I *was the hero that day. Well, I was going to be, if the Box hadn't intervened. My intentions were good, and that has to count for something. So... maybe I can do this. I've played difficult roles before.*

Coop stopped pacing and realized Jess had sat at the edge of the bed, just below Tycho's feet. She looked about to speak, but he held up a hand and stopped her. "I haven't figured out how to dialogue as soliloquy."

The look of total confusion on Jess' face made him feel a bit better.

"Come on, Jess, you must know that old joke? 'I'm not schizophrenic. And neither am I'?"

She frowned at him.

"What? That's funny."

"No, Mr. Cooper, it's not. Certainly not under the circumstances. Plus, it perpetuates a common misconception about psychology. Multiple personality disorder is not categorized under schizophrenia."

"It's not?"

"No. Schizophrenia involves hallucinations, confusion, delusions, sometimes movement disorders—"

He cut her off. "Okay, whatever. I think you just have no sense of humor, and that is a major disorder in my book. Anyway, my point is... You need to understand that I'm going to be talking to myself a lot going forward."

"Why?"

He sighed. She had book smarts, no question, but Jess' common sense was lacking. "So I can talk to Dyrk."

"What do you want to tell him?"

«Yes, what do you want to tell me?»

"Just this. I'm in, Dyrk. I'm ready to start acting like the heroes I've spent my life pretending to be. Now, how do we save Potato?"

CHAPTER THREE

Madam Zana trotted lightly through her parlor, a spacious room with velvet wallpaper that jammed most electronic signals even as it whispered two-century-old piano jazz from Earth's Crescent City. A light fragrance of jasmine floated in the air. Polished wood with velvet cushions and pillows defined the sittable furniture, and end tables bearing tiny hand-painted seascapes and replica oil lamps added to the surreal ambiance of the room. Zana had no idea if any of it was accurate, but she liked to think so. She nodded absently to the handful of her girls who lounged, awaiting clients. Most of them were human, but her establishment was no stranger to xenons, whether clientele or merchandise. She nodded once to the senior-most girl on duty and once to the bartender/bouncer, a signal that she was not to be disturbed, and slipped through a curtained alcove.

Once inside, a quick tap of a wall switch activated her suite of security measures. Her safe room had been a gift from her benefactor and would remain standing even if the spaceport itself were blown away. On the surface of it, that kind of durability was silly, but it was a cultural thing. Cormyrians only felt complete knowing they had access to a safe space somewhere. It didn't have to make sense. When she'd negotiated for the wholly impractical alcove as part of the house she ran, her patron had granted the request without consideration of the cost. She owed him for that and much more, and she was always pleased when the opportunity to repay some of that debt presented itself—as it had moments earlier in the so-called Ambassadorial Room.

She bypassed her usual communication array and selected a dedicated line. "Alhiz'khlo'tam, this is Zana. Are you available?"

A voice like the purr of a cat answered at once, attentive but sleepy at the same time. "I'm always available for you, dear Zana. What do you have for me?"

"A pair of idiots. Well, three, actually, but one appears incapacitated. They showed up at my doorstep, and not for any of my house's usual services."

"Human then?"

"Oh yes," Zana reported.

"Details?"

"The quick ones are an elderly male and a much younger female. The latter looks to have medical expertise. The third human is another female, younger than the first and likely her patient. I believe they're the 'thieves and terrorists' that have the Box up in arms."

"Interesting. And what do they seek?"

"The usual. Discreet passage off Titan."

"Interesting," repeated the voice. "The Box appear to be roused to action by whatever has happened."

Zana frowned at that. "You don't think they're bluffing? About leaving, I mean?"

"They don't have the imagination to bluff. They'll go if they don't get what they want. The question is how much damage they'll do along the way, and how I can best take advantage of the circumstances. As always, chaos breeds opportunity for those prepared to seize it. Which means it behooves me to help your guests."

"I assumed as much. I'm preparing to send them to Hugo's. Will that work for you?"

"Perfectly. Do you have images you can send along? Too many humans look alike to me."

"Of course. I've had them on surveillance since they arrived." She tapped the communication console and scrolled through a list of rooms and screens displaying their respective occupants until a view from the Ambassadorial Room appeared on the display. "Forwarding the data now."

"Thank you, Zana. You've done well. Please extend your every hospitality to these guests for the duration. Any humans who can annoy the Box to such an extent are people I want to cultivate and likely aid. I'll be in touch."

CHAPTER FOUR

Coop left Jess with Tycho. The doctor had Zana's tablet running a constant search of the newsfeed for relevant keywords and further developments. Coop—with Dyrk along for the ride—borrowed a hooded sweatshirt from the bordello's proprietress and skulked into the maze of alleys, side streets, tunnels, and underground levels that made up the city surrounding the spaceport. Beyond eventually trying to meet up with Zana's contact, he didn't have a specific destination in mind. Dyrk had said something about reconnoitering the area, so they wandered while the viral echo compiled some sort of tally of available resources. Coop also wanted to talk to Dyrk without Jess staring at him like he was a crazy person just because he was talking to a voice in his head. *Sheesh.*

Coop pulled the hood up and hunched his head down. He'd played a couple of street toughs in the early days of his film career, and he knew how to make himself look unapproachable. It wasn't natural for a man with his extra dose of charisma, but such was the depth of his commitment to his craft. Talking to himself as he walked was easier than focusing his thoughts enough to speak to Dyrk in his head, and the muttering added a nice degree of crazy to the role he projected.

"So, Dyrk. It's time for you to level with me. How good are you? I mean, are you like James Bond good? Or are you all talk? And don't bullshit me, okay? I need you to be honest. We've got a lot riding on this."

«Well, Ben. I've been thinking about that question. And the answer is, I don't know.»

"That is not at all what I was looking for, Dyrk. You're the one that insisted we stay and rescue Potato. Dig deep and come up with more than 'I don't know.'"

Dyrk protested, *«Hold on. Hold on. I'm not saying I don't have skills. I have tons of skills. I'm like a ninja, but better looking. I can shoot. I can drive. I can fight. These are skills I know. And there are a lot more where those came from. The problem is, I don't know what I don't know.»*

"Yeah, you're going to need to explain that for me."

«Think about it, Ben. I'm a one-dimensional character. I'm an action hero and therefore awesome by definition. Epic, even. But that's all I am, the action part. I have no depth. I've no relationships. I don't know history or context. You've had a real life. You've loved and lost. You've had friendships. You've experienced things. Sure, clearly a lot of it sucked, and we both know a lot of that was your own fault.»

"I think that's a bit harsh—"

Dyrk ignored the attempted interruption. *«I've never done any of that. I'm just... What did you call me? A viral echo? I'm based on thousands of hours of film. So, yes, I admit that it could be a problem, especially as regards our mission of rescuing Potato and departing Titan.»*

Coop sought greater. "Okay, so, if I'm understanding right, you have skills, but you don't have any judgment. You're lacking any experience to tell you when to do something or when not to do it."

«Exactly. Plus, I don't know how to act with people. I'm trying out different styles as I go along.»

"Is that why you sound different now than when you talked with Jess?"

«Well, yes. She's a physician and a scientist. That's how you're supposed to talk to highly educated professionals, isn't it?» Dyrk asked.

Coop shrugged as he continued his way along yet another seedy side street. "I don't know. Characters in films may do that. I've had a wide range of dialogue styles over the years, but in real life I tend to talk to everyone pretty much the same."

«Is that what normal human beings do?»

Coop laughed. "Dyrk, there is no such thing as a normal human being. Trust me on that one. But the good news is, acting like a normal person is something I know how to do."

«Then why don't you do it more often?»

"Excuse me?"

Dyrk brushed it off. *«Never mind. I just don't want my shortcomings to sabotage things.»*

"I get it. Just so you know, doubt and uncertainty are a regular part of the human condition. When I worked on the stage, we didn't get another take. We had one shot every night to get it right for our audience. When opening night came and the curtain rose, if you've learned your lines, found your motivation, rehearsed for hundreds of hours to hone your performance, well, you can only do your best. And if it's great, the reviews may still kill you."

«Is that supposed to be helpful? Because as pep talks go, it's pretty bad. Do my best? That's going to be cold comfort to Potato if my best isn't good enough.»

"Potato is a lump," Coop pointed out. "It's not going to know or care one way or the other. But more importantly, stop catastrophizing."

Coop paused at an intersection. The last narrow passage he'd taken had left him at a junction with a much larger and more crowded tunnel full of shops and restaurants. Robotic pallet-loaders zipped by, and a swarm of humanity—and xenonity—went about their business, shopping and transporting goods. Rather than rush into the throng where his one-sided conversation might draw too much attention, he opted to hang back, lean against the conduit piping, and watch the scene unfold while he finished his chat with Dyrk.

"Listen up. There is no telling what's going to happen to us. We can agree on that. But there isn't much sense in drowning in pessimism, either. Imagining all the ways things can go wrong is useful for planning purposes but it does nothing but hold you back when it comes time for action. If you need to engage your imagination, stop focusing on the negative and start imagining success. It'll be easier on both of us."

«*Wrong, Ben!*» Dyrk argued. «*The negative is where the danger lies. It's what keeps me on edge. It's what keeps me sharp and motivated. Danger and fear make me stronger and better. The aroma of risk is like a perfumed bosom to my senses.*»

"Really? A perfumed bosom? Even I wouldn't say that."

«*Didn't you get butterflies in your stomach before live performances?*»

"Sure, Dyrk."

«*Even the ones you'd done successfully a dozen times?*»

"Yeah, I guess," Coop admitted.

«*Why?*»

"Because when you perform live, anything can happen."

«*Exactly. And that rush, that edge, kept you on your toes, right?*»

Coop thought back across countless performances. "Huh. I guess it did."

«*Well, that's my point. I need to be my best if we're going to pull this off. To be my best, I need to feel the anxiety. I need the rush.*»

"That's not healthy," Coop observed.

«Coop, I'm the personification of action movies. I wouldn't know 'healthy' if it bit you in the ass. Now, what do you say we go get a drink and see if we can gather some intel along the way?»

"Now you're talking my language."

CHAPTER FIVE

As soon as Mr. Cooper and his new alter-ego left the room, Jessica went to work. All of what Dyrk had said made sense, more or less. They had to get off Titan and they had to avoid the Box, but those weren't areas where her expertise would be much use. She still wasn't fully convinced that Dyrk was as real as he thought he was, but at least he had a plan and the willingness to run with it. What Dyrk didn't seem to appreciate, either generally or from a self-interest perspective, was her need to figure out precisely what was going on with the virus! She had never, ever imagined it developing as a sapient individual. She had most certainly not foreseen it...*hijacking* another living being's central nervous system as it appeared to be doing to Mr. Cooper.

But clearly, it had. The evidence was irrefutable. It had happened right in front of her over just a couple of days. Which meant all the pieces were also there. She just had to identify them and put them together. Damn if Dyrk wasn't right again, albeit for entirely different reasons: she was going to need Potato.

Jessica started pacing. Again.

"Okay, Tycho," she said as she passed the comatose young

woman for the fifth time. "I just need you to listen while I think out loud."

Predictably, Tycho did not respond.

"Perfect. Thank you. Okay, Jessica, think. Start with the most likely explanations and proceed to the however-impossible-it-might-just-be-true. So... Is it possible that Mr. Cooper is faking this whole Dyrk thing? Sure, it's possible. He's an actor and a bit of a nut. If he can pretend to be a normal human being on occasion, he can certainly act as if he's under the effect or influence of another personality. But why would he? Right, he wouldn't. He's scared, desperate to get off this moon and to somewhere safe. He knows he needs to escape. And while he might be an actor, I doubt he's capable of dreaming this whole thing up. Originality doesn't seem to be his forte."

Jessica looked at Tycho for confirmation. "Right." She resumed pacing.

"Mr. Cooper has been under a lot of stress. A lot. A chunk of that is my fault, from injecting him with the virus that... created Dyrk, to the initial tests I put him through. It's possible I wasn't as kind to him as I could have been. But in fairness to me, the man is patently ridiculous. He's a chauvinistic dinosaur. And..." Jessica took a deep breath. Despite a lifetime of experience with guilt and self-recrimination, her conscience reminded her that this wasn't the time for blaming others. With an act of will, she redirected her thoughts to the real problem.

"Focus, Jessica. So, we know Mr. Cooper has been under a lot of emotional strain. He is an older man with the life experience and baggage that age brings, as well as an addictive personality and decades of substance abuse. He has been properly medicated since arriving on Titan, but he has also been withdrawing from alcohol, which is known to cause delirium and other psychotic symptoms. And yet, my workup of him didn't reveal any symptoms of acute alcohol withdrawal. So, while it is a possible explanation, it's at best only a plausible and partial one."

Jessica completed another lap. "However, at the same time, he's been suffering the after-effects of null-space syndrome. That's a possibly massive contributing factor, one which could interact with his other issues to produce this situation. Unfortunately, there's nothing in the database about null-space syndrome and alcohol withdrawal. Apparently, there aren't enough stupid people out there to provide a body of knowledge on the subject. Still, if I'm being fair, that combination has to also remain a plausible explanation. But is it the most likely one?"

She paused and glanced at the young woman in the bed, projecting an answer onto her silence.

"No? Well, thanks, I agree with you. It's too unnecessarily complicated to leave in play. Occam's Razor for the win."

Jessica chewed on her fingernails as she continued to pace. She occasionally spit them into the bathroom trash as she passed by on her brief circuit.

"All right, Tycho. What does that leave? What if Mr. Cooper is telling the truth. Not just the truth as he believes it, but the actual answer for his symptoms. Would it explain his lack of memory? Yes. Would it explain the skills and knowledge he utilized that he has no other acceptable explanation for? Yes. Would it account for all of the… weird stuff that is going on with him physically and cognitively? I mean, not his usual weird stuff. The new things. Yes."

Jessica ended her pacing and stared off in the direction of the bathroom without really seeing it. She focused on some intangible notion that hovered before her mind's eye, letting it hang there and captivate her thinking as time hung suspended. When she resumed speaking several minutes later, it was as if all doubt had vanished and the truth lay bare before her, unsettling and bizarre as it might be.

"Tycho, I hate to say this, but I think Mr. Cooper has been invaded by an alien body snatcher. And it… he… Dyrk may be our only hope of getting out of this mess alive."

If Tycho had heard and understood anything Jessica had said, she managed to contain her sense of trepidation and continued to provide absolutely no observable response. Jessica spent another moment admiring the woman's consistency and then picked up the tablet Madam Zana had left. She checked for any relevant updates and, finding none, set it aside in favor of her medical tablet she'd taken from the Box ranch. Having accepted Dyrk's existence, a series of questions had instantly presented themselves and she was already formulating experiments to answer them with the resources available to her.

A chill raced up and down her spine, and goose bumps ran along her arms. Her breathing shifted, becoming shallow and rapid. A feeling of inexplicable trepidation threatened to drown her. What if she couldn't do this? What if all she could contribute was an endless list of inane questions? What if her own research, the work that had created Dyrk, remained impenetrable to her?

And then all that doubt fell away, driven off by the simple habit of doing the things she knew how to do. Her fingers danced across the screen, and she began crafting those questions into testable hypotheses. The cool logic of science calmed her. That calm added to her focus and let her fine-tune her hypothesis testing. She was back in her element, in control.

"Perfect." She placed her fingers against her wrist to check her pulse.

Seconds ticked by as Jessica monitored her vitals. Her breathing slowed. Her heart rate dropped, and all the anxiety that had sent her pacing had vanished. "Weird."

BAM! BAM! BAM!

The door shook as someone knocked on it with a vigor that made the madam's earlier visit seem like the touch of a gentle rain.

CHAPTER SIX

At Dyrk's prodding, Coop meandered through the increasingly seedy tunnels of the city beneath the spaceport. The worst portion had acquired the colorful name of the Warrens, and he tried to imagine rabbits hippity-hopping through the layered filth that defined the place. He came up short and just kept walking. Peter Cottontail had no business being on Titan anyway.

Coop stopped in front of a rough-looking bar. The front door was made of mismatched metal rods welded together. Graffiti and suspicious-looking stains adorned the façade and likely accounted for the smell of urine— and worse—that wafted up to Coop's nose. At least it wasn't the bar he'd torn apart a few days before. That would have been a bad idea. The neon sign over this door read "Hugo's."

"You're sure this is the place Madam Zana was talking about?" Coop asked.

«We're here because we followed the directions she provided. What's the problem?»

"I don't know. I mean, I know we're looking for a guy to get us off Titan illicitly, but I guess I was hoping for a place where we wouldn't get stabbed."

«Ben, we ain't in Casablanca, *this isn't Rick's, and you most certainly aren't Humphrey Bogart.»*

"That wasn't necessary," Coop objected.

«My bad. I'm just trying to make you appreciate that when you need underhanded, illegal stuff done, you go to where the criminals are.»

"Congress?"

«Ha! Good one. But no. You know what I mean. Now get in there and turn on the Ben Cooper charm. We need new identities and intel. You're the movie star. Make it happen!»

"All right. Sure. I can do this." Coop stood up straight and put on his best approachable-but-don't-fuck-with-me face.

«Does that hurt?»

"Does what hurt?"

«Making your face do that. Like you're having a bad reaction to tacos.»

"I'm getting in character," Coop explained. "Don't mock my technique. Now, are you going to shut up and let me do this?"

«Sure. But not without a little bit of ridicule. No, don't argue. Just get in there and let me feed you lines, okay? This isn't the Beverly Wilshire. You're in my element now.»

"Your element is on a couch in front of a dozen video monitors."

«Now, that *wasn't necessary.»*

"Yeah, well, I'm not sorry."

«Whatever. I'm not keeping score. Let's roll.»

Coop shrugged his shoulders to loosen up and walked into the bar. Dyrk's crack about the Beverly Wilshire notwithstanding, a bar was a bar, and he'd frequented a great many of them over the years. The unmistakable stench of stale beer and staler bodies greeted him as he surveyed this one, and he admitted maybe Dyrk *was* right after all. The place wasn't much to look at, as if someone had taken a long corridor and decided to throw in a few tables and chairs and serve drinks. Odd as that was, the clientele was even worse.

"Damn," Coop muttered. "It's like a miniature version of the Mos Eisley Cantina from *Star Wars*."

«That was a great movie.»

"I know, right?"

That simple glance convinced Coop this was the premiere spot for any down-on-their-luck non-humans to lose themselves in self-medication. He didn't know a lot about the assorted xenon species, but he knew sleazy when he saw it. These folks, xenon *and* humans, had sleaze oozing from their ears and a few other alien orifices that he could see but didn't want to know anything about. In the case of one human who blessedly had his back to Coop, the stuff seeping from his ears looked more like a bacterial infection. The actor shuddered. Still, in the grand scheme of things it was no worse than the wrap party in that abandoned sewage treatment plant in Bakersfield after they'd finished filming *Flying Wombats of Panama*. It was all relative and perspective was everything. He'd learned that in his first year on stage, and it was the key to getting through most any situation. With that maxim in mind, Coop moved confidently toward the far end of the bar.

It was slow going down the repurposed corridor. The bar and its occupants were to his right, and there wasn't much space to work with. It dawned on him that maybe, just maybe, the bar had started life as a shipping container. Or maybe not. First, why would someone bury a shipping container underneath the spaceport? Also, even a shipping container would have had more charm. The air tasted stale. Then again, it was probably a mercy that whatever toxins existed throughout the bar weren't circulating, let alone blending into ever more vile mixtures. Coop moved in and out of different varieties of stagnant, putrid air until finally he reached the last empty stool in the place, sitting between two other patrons.

On his left sat one of the few human customers. The man had a row of empty beer glasses in front of him and a totally disinterested look plastered to his bearded face as he stared at a tiny wrist screen. The tinny voices of a decade-old soap opera were almost comprehensible. He wore sweat-stained coveralls with "Doug" stitched over the left breast.

He looked like a Doug.

To Coop's right sat a xenon, a member of one of the few races he could identify: the Clustera. Coop didn't know a damn thing about the alien race, where they came from, or why any of them bothered visiting the solar system. Why would he? He only knew what everyone knew from the media. The Clustera were one of the most human-looking species in the galaxy, which naturally had spawned all kinds of conspiracy theories. Not that they actually looked human, but compared to other xenon, like the whorehouse madam for example, they were maybe distant cousins. Very distant. This Clusteran looked like a typical sort, complete with elongated ears, midnight-black skin, and a towering seven-foot stature. The Clustera only passed for regular human people to other xenons, and even then, only from afar.

This particular alien looked well-dressed. More importantly, when held against the standard established by the other patrons, he seemed clean and lucid. He even smelled good.

«Is that Aqua Di Giò? I love that stuff.»

Coop ignored Dyrk's comment and gave the alien a small nod as he sat down next to him. The Clusteran responded with a crooked but seemingly genuine smile.

«I don't think Doug's going to be much help. But the tall alien has some expensive bling, and did you notice how he's positioned himself at the very end of the bar to keep a watchful eye on the front door. That's the mark of a pro. He practically screams otherworldly mobster. This is so awesome. Let's start with him.»

Coop nodded and turned to face the alien.

"Nice place."

The Clusteran snorted in a very human sign of amusement. "You must not get out much." The alien's voice was surprisingly deep. Coop admired a good, deep voice. He knew a dozen actors who had used just such a voice as the foundation for very lucrative careers.

"Last time I went drinking, the bar got destroyed in a brawl. It seemed safer to start with a place that already looked like a bomb hit it."

"Indeed." The alien cast a pointed glance around the bar. "I hope you don't make a habit of demolishing watering holes. *Businessmen* such as myself need office space, and it can be hard to come by on this orange rock."

«Business! Did you hear that? He said he's a 'businessman' just like a gangster. This is good!»

Coop sighed. "What kind of business are you in, Mister…"

"You couldn't pronounce it. Just call me Al."

«Al? That is not a good gangster name. Well, I guess it could be. Maybe it's short for Alphonse or something. Or an homage to Al Capone? That would be epic. I like this guy.»

Coop's neck and back felt tight. He rubbed his temples. "Al, I'm… Ben Cooper."

The Clusteran took a small sip of his drink. "I know. Our mutual friend told me to watch out for you."

«You think this is the guy Madam Zana mentioned? He seems a little out of her league. Then again, why would that kind of guy hang out in a rat hole like this? Something's off. Unless... Maybe he deliberately wants us to think something's off, and it's some kind of test? Whoa!»

Internally, Coop growled at Dyrk, *Will you shut the hell up?*

"Okay. Well, our *friend* said you could help us with some business."

"Well, Cooper, I'm in the import-export business. Is that what you're looking for?"

"Mostly the export side of things, actually."

"Ah. I see. Would your...*cargo*...be going out into the greater galaxy or inbound to Earth?"

"The latter," specified Coop. "Earth."

Before he could elaborate, a fat man with a bushy unibrow and an unwashed apron interrupted from the other side of the bar.

"Hey sweetheart, are you gonna order a drink or keep hitting on my customers? This is MY business, honey. So, buy something or get out before I toss your pretty ass out of an airlock."

«Kick his ass, Seabass!»

Coop felt Dyrk chomping at some kind of mental bit as if he wanted to start another barroom brawl. It was all Coop could do to shove him down. "Vodka and tonic, please. And don't shake it. You'll crack the ice. If the ice is cracked, I'm sending it back."

The bartender huffed and prepared the drink. Coop winced as the man's greasy hands wrapped around the neck of a bottle. The sound of a chair sliding across the floor caused him to turn back toward the Clusteran.

Al had stood and extended one of his long-fingered hands to Cooper. "I believe I've heard of you, Coop, and have a grasp of the situation you're in. But don't worry. Knowing things is part of my job. I can assist you with your shipping needs, but it would help me to know if your former employers will be aware of your...cargo's departure?"

"I sure as hell hope not."

The alien nodded in understanding.

"When would your cargo like to leave Titan, Cooper?"

"Ideally, on the passenger ship next week." Coop shook Al's proffered hand.

The alien nodded. "How many passengers?"

"Three. One of them isn't, uh, ambulatory."

"So I've heard. It won't be cheap. And let me be clear, if I invest my time into a business deal with you, there is no backing out."

Coop recognized the threat. He'd been threatened a lot in his life, by other actors, assistant directors, gaffers, catering staff, a few enraged husbands, and even a couple Christmas elves when he'd mistakenly wound up taking a job as a department store Santa early on in his career. A threat by an overly tall alien was new. Second thoughts bubbled up in his mind even as a shiver of fear ran down his spine.

It was all Dyrk needed to pull himself into the control seat.

«Not to worry, Al. I'll have cash and some very rare intellectual property to offer in payment. It should be more than enough for a businessman with your connections.»

The Clusteran lifted his chin, catching the attention of the other human down the bar. "Doug, it appears I will require your services. Please keep yourself available."

Doug looked up from his wrist screen, smiled, and wiped his hands on his greasy shirt. "You got it, Mr. Al. Just let me know when and where, and I'm there."

The alien nodded and returned his attention back to Dyrk. "Good. Doug is very capable and technically gifted. He's also possessed of some very…uncommon tastes, which in turn makes compensating him and guaranteeing his silence very easy. Now, I will, of course, need to know more about this *intellectual property*. But not now. This is my business address. Call me." Al handed over a black business card with both a Titanian and a Solar comm extension on it.

«Will do, Al,» confirmed Dyrk. «Good meeting you.»

The alien turned and walked out of the bar.

Coop found himself back in control of his body. Relief flooded him.

«*That went well.*»

"Did it?"

Doug jerked his head toward Coop. "Are you talking to me?"

Coop ignored him, which seemed to suit Doug just fine, as he returned to the pedestrian drama unfolding on his wrist screen. Coop went back to focusing on what Dyrk was saying.

«Sure. He knows what you need. He was waiting for us like Zana said he'd be. A guy like that probably knows exactly who you are and why you want off this stupid moon. No doubt he has a shadowy network of henchmen, pickpockets, and roustabouts that provide him intel from all over the station.»

"Did you actually say 'roustabouts'? And 'pickpockets'? This isn't a Charles Dickens book.'"

«Who? At any rate, yes. I did. Those words are perfectly legit under the circumstances.»

"Maybe three hundred years ago."

«I'm the films that Dr. Acorns showed to Potato. Wait, were there even films that long ago? Stop distracting me, Ben. Do you appreciate what this means? Al knows we're expecting to return to the ranch, and by extension he knows that the tech we're offering will be something we've stolen from the Box.»

"So?"

«So he will damn sure know how much it's worth.»

"I hope you're right."

«I am.»

The bartender returned with Coop's drink and an abundance of body odor.

"Thank you," Coop muttered, but the man just stood there and glared until Coop slid a credit chip across the counter. The bartender swept it up in a meaty palm and, without so much as a backward glance, departed to check on his other customers.

Coop stared down at the drink but didn't reach for it.

«Is something wrong with your drink? I'm sure the vodka has killed off anything that might have been living on the glass.»

"It's not that. I'm just thinking back to what you told Jess about being accountable. For years, I haven't been. The booze was a great excuse. For everything. I've used it as a crutch and a shield, never letting anybody get close. I've used it to stay numb and to rationalize behavior I knew was wrong at the time but went and did anyway. But I've been given a second chance. And I'm starting to think that has to mean making different choices."

Coop drummed his fingers for a minute before he dropped another credit chip on the bar and shoved his untouched glass over to Doug. Then he stood and exited the shit-hole without another glance at the drink.

CHAPTER SEVEN

Traversing yet another urine-soaked tunnel and a debris-laden ramp, Coop eventually arrived at the main promenade of the spaceport. It was almost early afternoon, and the delicious aroma of roasting meat set his stomach to rumbling. The heavenly scent blotted out any concern about what kind of meat it might be or how it had come to be on Titan.

Dyrk remained blessedly silent, allowing Coop to ruminate over the sudden changes in his life as he paused at a couple of vendors. He bought an assortment of meats on sticks. They were all glorious. He hadn't realized how damn hungry he'd been.

«*It all tastes like chicken,*» Dyrk complained.

"What?"

«*The meat. It all tastes like chicken. Isn't that weird? We're a gazillion miles from a real source of animal protein, so assuming it's not just some vat-grown soy derivative, it all has to be brought here at great expense.*»

"And?"

«*And if you're going to go to all that trouble, wouldn't you want to make it taste different?*» Dyrk pointed out.

"I thought they had different flavors. One was clearly some kind of lamb."

«Sure it was. Have you seen a goat around here? Different flavors of chicken, my butt. Stupidly expensive chicken.»

"First off, goat isn't lamb. Right? Anyway, did you enjoy it?"

«Oh, heck yes!»

"Then shut up." Coop stopped in the middle of the promenade as an uneasy feeling took over. "You can taste what I taste?"

«Um, hello? We're sharing the same body. I have access to all your senses.»

"All of them?"

«Yes, sir. I sure do.»

"Whoa. That could get…awkward."

«Tell me about it. I know I have limited human experience, but I already know there are some smells that I could live without. I'm not judging, but your diet needs work.»

He shook his head, hoping it would clear away the thought his new mental roommate had dropped there. They had more important things to deal with, and honestly, some of the details really creeped him out.

"So, Dyrk. If we somehow survive the next few days and by some miracle make it off this damn moon, what do you want to do?"

«Oh, that's easy. Everything.»

Coop blanched. "That's a lot of territory to cover. Could you narrow it down for me?"

«Well, like I said. I haven't experienced much of anything. Nada. Zip. Zero. I want to have real, first-hand experiences of all the best stuff.»

"And what do you consider the best stuff?"

«I don't know for sure, but I have some theories.»

"Go on." Coop spoke with more than a little trepidation. It had just occurred to him that unless Jess figured out a way to transplant the viral echo, he'd be the one on the hook for Dyrk's buffet of experiences.

«I want to see and do all the stuff I haven't seen in my films. I want to form my own memories. I'd like to meet people and make relationships. Good ones and bad ones. I'd like them to be real people. Not the kind that show up in action movies. I'd like to form real connections. Yeah, that's it. I want to travel to Los Angeles and meet real, normal people like you.»

Coop did not have the heart to explain that L.A. wasn't the best place to meet normal people.

«I guess what I want is...depth. Does that make sense?»

"Not only does it make sense, but it sounds like a very healthy concept of the human experience."

«Yeah? Thanks, Ben. So, what do you want to do when we finish up with this adventure?»

"Adventure? I'll leave that one alone. I came here because Scatola promised me a big-budget action flick. A film where I could finally show the world the full range of my talents and put an end to the lies and rumors that killed my career. Maybe even make a comeback. But somehow, that doesn't feel very important now. And listening to your goals makes me wonder if I've been doing it all wrong. Maybe I should be focusing on the relationships in my life too. The depth, as you put it."

Coop began walking again. He had no destination in mind, but a sense of purpose fueled his steps.

Dyrk sensed that Ben needed some time to think, and besides, all the old guy had to do was walk to where Dyrk instructed him. So, the alien took the opportunity to sink back away from the actor's consciousness and do a bit of his own rumination.

Life and death was kind of a big deal, Dyrk decided. One that seemed to require a lot of effort and energy. He knew it showed up as a subplot or theme in plenty of the movies that defined him, but that didn't mean he'd ever really experienced or understood it. Usually, people just switched to a new scene, and when they did, they had recovered. It never took very long. Except, since he'd come to consciousness inside Ben, he had learned that human bodies had all kinds of needs and frailties that rarely, if ever, came out on the big screen. Even when they did, it wasn't nearly in proportion to the amount of time they required to heal.

They needed to eat. They needed to sleep. They used the bathroom all the time. What was that about, anyway? Humans never used the bathroom in the movies unless they wanted to get ambushed while standing at a urinal. Bathrooms were places to be avoided at all costs. But it was more than just that. All these human needs and urges distracted from important stuff like action, adventure, and rescuing people. Dyrk was only a few days old, but he already found it all very disconcerting.

On the flip side, he had begun to appreciate a whole new world of sensation. Human bodies were plugged into everything. They took in sights, sounds, smells, and more all at the same time. The full range of Ben's sensory apparati made no sense whatsoever. It was an overwhelming maelstrom that constantly threatened to overload. How were you supposed to know what to filter out of your attention and what to focus on? Though he hadn't admitted it to Ben, the taste of those meat sticks hung in his memory, demanding equal time alongside the new sights and sounds of everything around his host. It boggled his mind, scary and thrilling all at once.

Still, he was learning to handle it, even if it was all a bit much. Adapting quickly was part of what defined him. Truth be told, he was enjoying the hell out of it.

«Maybe that's the key, Dyrk old boy. Relax and enjoy life. That must be how humans do it. After all, they'd go crazy if they didn't. Right?»

Yeah, that seemed right.

CHAPTER EIGHT

Jessica did her best not to jump out of her skin and instead slapped both hands over her mouth to stifle her second inclination, which was to scream. She looked right. She looked left. The tiny room offered nowhere to go and nowhere to hide. She dropped to all fours to see if she could crawl under the bed, only to discover the mattress sat on a platform that rested directly on the floor. Not that it really mattered. She couldn't hide Tycho.

"Dammit," she whispered.

The doctor turned to face the door and then bent further, pressing the side of her head to the floor. The position allowed her to peek under the door, though the gap was incredibly slight. With the exception of airlocks, doors on Titan were never flush with the floor. She didn't know why—maybe it was because of the airlocks, and people wanted to know at a glance which exits led to an atmospheric seal and which didn't. She could make out shadows moving in the hallway, but not any real detail, just what she imagined were shoes—or at least a pair of feet. She had no idea who or what had knocked, but they hadn't left yet.

Was it Madam Zana? Not likely. She'd announce herself. Could it be the Box? Had they found her already? That would be a disaster. No, no, no.

Whoever or whatever it was, she needed to let Mr. Cooper know. It wasn't likely he'd be able to help, but maybe Dyrk could...

Jessica sat up and tapped away at her tablet, opening a tab to the public message board where Dyrk had created a fake account.

SNICK

A key inserted itself into the lock.

Jessica leapt to her feet. Her toes landed lightly on the dirty floor and she tossed her tablet onto the bed next to Tycho, who hadn't shown any concern at their approaching doom.

The doorknob turned. Slowly. Quietly.

This isn't good.

The doctor moved swiftly and silently across the room. She positioned herself to one side of the door, in the gap between the wall and the point where the door would stop. She prayed the intruder wouldn't be able to see her.

Her heartbeat thundered in her ears. Her breathing sounded ragged and way too loud. It was impossible to believe the intruder wouldn't hear it. She held her breath and prayed.

The door inched open, creaking as it arced further and further into the room.

Jessica's head pounded from the blood rushing to her brain.

She saw the tip of a man's dress shoe enter the room. A moment later, the rest of the man shuffled forward silently, moving cautiously into the room.

Every bone in Jessica's body told her to scream, that if ever there was a time to do so, this was it. Or better yet, forget screaming. She should run. Or maybe not run, maybe just bash the bastard over the head with the lamp on the nightstand.

Why didn't I grab the damn lamp?

Her eyes cast about the room, searching for another potential weapon. But there was nothing. Nothing that wouldn't force her to expose herself to her assailant.

Time had slowed to a crawl. She caught a glimpse of the man's nose and then his chin as they passed the edge of the open door. Her own nostrils recoiled as the scent of cheap cologne hit her. A low, über-disgusting chuckle emanated from the man's throat. It was guttural and predatory. It was the laugh of a man on the hunt. A man who had found his prey.

Jessica looked over and saw Tycho laying helplessly on the bed, young and attractive despite her coma, helpless and clothed in a simple hospital gown. That sight had made the man laugh. Her foot lashed out and struck her side of the door, and Jessica gave in to the urge to scream. Not from the growing panic that had all but paralyzed her a moment ago, but from sheer outrage.

"Not. Today!" she shouted.

The door slammed into the man's face and crashed home with a satisfying *thwack* as he recoiled from it, then his head was bounced off the other side of the door frame. She followed up in a blind terror and threw her whole body against the door. The intruder's head was rocked again, and he crumpled to the floor in a heap. His tongue lolled out the side of his slackened mouth

Dr. Acorns leapt to the bed and stared down at the intruder lying supine with half his body still in the hallway. He was a small human male. Barely five-foot-four, probably in his forties, balding and with the beginning of a beer gut. His nose looked like it'd been broken before, perhaps more than once, and he had a large wart on the back of his right hand. But his clothes looked expensive and professional. Blood trickled from a small gash on his head, and he was clearly unconscious. But for how long?

Jessica tiptoed around Tycho and snatched the lamp off the table. She returned to her perch and held the light above her head. She remained like that for several seconds.

I must look like an idiot.

"You look like an idiot. Why are you standing there and what did you do to Mr. Henry?"

Madam Zana stood in the hallway just behind the intruder with her purple arms crossed over her chest. She looked imperious and none too pleased.

"Henry? Is that his name?" Jessica lowered the lamp and sheepishly hugged it to her chest.

"Yes. And he's one of my better, if more… varied, clients. Of course, he can afford it."

"Oh, right. Money. I suppose that explains it."

"Explains what?"

"Men with money find ways to buy access."

"I'm not following."

Jessica sighed. "He had a key. He unlocked the door and stood there, leering at my friend. He didn't know I was here, and I think he was going to…"

Zana shook her head. "Damn idiot. He probably copied these old analog keys. He's certainly used every room at some point. Well, don't worry yourself, dear. I'll take care of this."

Without another word, the alien leaned down and grabbed him by the hem of his trousers. She dragged him from the room and down the hall. A moment later, Jessica heard what she thought was the sound of Mr. Henry's head bouncing down the stairs one at a time.

Her legs were shaking, so she stepped off the bed and crossed to the door to close and lock it. Not that it had helped much with Mr. Henry. She sat in the chair, lowered the lamp to the floor, and breathed a sigh of relief.

A moment later, she closed her eyes and passed out before she could even rest her face in her hands.

CHAPTER NINE

Coop meandered down the bustling promenade with Dyrk riding mental shotgun. He needed time to think, and the crowd provided the white noise and anonymity he required.

"Dyrk, I have a question."

«Shoot, Ben!»

"Is it just me, or is it getting easier for us to co-exist?"

«Oh, it should be getting easier. I've been working on that.»

"What do you mean?"

«I've been making some changes, upgrading you so that it becomes easier for your body to accommodate a second mind. It isn't difficult, really. Just shuffling a few things around in your central nervous system. No biggie.»

"Um... Say what?"

«And speaking of moving things around, who the heck is this hot girl, Paige? She takes up a ton of space in here. You must think of her constantly. But I get it. She is an incredibly attractive young lady. Wow.»

Coop stopped walking. "Dyrk. Paige is my daughter. If you ever talk about her like that again—from inside my own brain no less—I will sit down and force you to watch a marathon of romantic comedies. Do I make myself clear?"

«Ben! Whoa! Slow your roll. There is no need for violence. Heck, as a prisoner in here, that could qualify as torture. I didn't know you had a daughter. My bad.»

Satisfied that his threat had hit home, Coop resumed his route. "Tell me more about how you're rearranging things."

«Well, it helps that you've been under plenty of stress. It gives me more fuel to work with. Basically, that stress empowers me to heal your body, wipe away the effects of aging, and provide some...general improvements.»

"Improvements? What could possibly need improving?"

«SMH, Ben.»

"Don't shake your head at me. Wait, it's my head anyway. Don't shake my head at me either."

«I won't. I'm too tired to exert control right now, anyway.»

"You get tired? I guess that kind of makes sense."

«Yep. It's sort of a pendulum. Right now, I'm coasting on the fumes of the adrenaline. When that wave crashes I'll go dormant and check out for a bit. But while I've got the fuel, I can be productive. So that's what I've been doing. Spending it in the short run because of the long-term benefits to us both. But eventually we'll find a balance. From the look of things, we have a long time ahead of us to figure these things out.»

"Okay. That helps. But, I have another question."

«Keep 'em coming.»

"How do you know all this stuff? I mean, how do you know how to do so much? I get that you've watched a lot of movies. But the actor just pretends to disarm the bomb. He doesn't actually know how to do it in real life. But you sure as hell have some admirable skills."

«Ah. Well, it's a little complicated, so I'll try to break it down so you can understand it.»

"Was that a dig?"

«Let it go, Ben. There are two types of knowledge for me. There is knowledge I have, and there is knowledge I have dedicated space for. If I watch somebody do a judo move, I can do it. I know how to move my body, so I can immediately apply that knowledge. And after I've approximated it once, I can fine-tune it and burn the muscle memory into this body. But if I watch somebody defuse a bomb, all I can do immediately is cut a wire. I don't know how the bomb works or how to decide which wire. But the thing is, my mind has slots for that information. All I have to do is get exposed to that knowledge, and the learning fills in the ready-made void.»

"So, if you read how to do something or someone explains it to you, you retain it?"

«Yep. If it is a skill I have a pre-made aptitude for.»

Coop stopped in the middle of the street and looked up at a sign above one of the nearby storefronts.

Titan Public Data Center

"Hey, Dyrk?"

«Yeah?»

"By any chance, do you have one of your knowledge slots set aside for hacking?"

«Just call me Crash Override, Ben. I like where your head's at.»

Cooper stepped into the data center, glanced around, and approached an open terminal.

CHAPTER TEN

Jessica's eyes opened, and she shook off the effects of an unexpected nap. "Whoa. What the hell happened?"

A moment passed before she stood slowly. "I guess I needed the rest." She stretched her back and returned to her routine of slow pacing. Her mind cleared with each step.

The doctor glanced at Tycho's prone form and let her thoughts wander as her feet clopped out a soothing cadence. Minutes passed, and the germ of an idea took shape. She rolled the result around in her mind, examining it from every side. Each footfall corresponded to another critical consideration, some aspect of the idea rejected or replaced until she realized it was as good as it needed to be.

Jess stopped and sat next to Tycho on the bed. She took the younger woman's hand in her own and placed her fingers over Tycho's pulse.

"Your heart rate is perfectly steady, Tycho. Not a hint of stress or strain. Must be nice. Sorry, I don't really mean that," she apologized.

Jessica ruminated for a minute as her thumb traced back and forth over Tycho's wrist.

"Okay, Tycho, here's the thing. You can't sense most external stimuli, and even the sounds you're able to hear aren't being actively processed in any conscious way. You don't experience emotional stress in your current state, nor are you feeling any physical pain. What all this means—if I'm correct about the norepinephrine acting as a catalyst—is the virus can't help you the way it's been helping Mr. Cooper. There's just no way to put you in that fight-or-flight state to trigger it and start it healing you. Unless…"

Jessica stood and went back to pacing, still speaking out loud to Tycho.

"Unless we can help you by helping the virus. Maybe we can nudge it in the right direction with a less obvious approach. Yeah, maybe…" Jessica picked up the tablet and opened up a new message screen. Her fingers flew and sent a note to Madam Zana.

A few minutes later, much sooner than Jessica expected, a gentle knock came at the door.

"Madam Zana?"

"Yes, dear. I have the things you asked for."

Jessica opened the door, but not before she peeked underneath to confirm the presence of purple feet. She took the package from the madam, who had the good grace to ask no questions. As Jessica thanked her and closed the door, she realized the madam had probably made stranger deliveries in her establishment.

Jess sat next to Tycho and opened the small duffel bag her host had delivered. She withdrew a pair of headphones and set them on the bed. Next, she pulled out a small bottle of epinephrine, a digital vitals monitor, and a pack of syringes. Her tablet could have tracked Tycho's vital signs, but having a dedicated device would leave the doctor free to use her own tablet for other things. She hooked up Tycho to the monitor, ran a quick test to confirm it worked, and set a baseline reading for her patient. She tied off Tycho's arm and applied a syringe to the bottle of epinephrine, flicking a few drops off the end of the needle when she was done.

"All right, Tycho, the plan is to see if we can fool your sympathetic nervous system into kicking things off." She inserted the needle into the comatose woman's arm and flinched. "I know you're probably not feeling this, but I hate sticking people." Jessica pressed the plunger and watched the adrenal solution enter Tycho's vein. As she withdrew the needle, Tycho responded with a reflexive twinge. The unexpected movement caused Jessica to fumble the syringe. The sharp point gouged a furrow across her own finger, and as she bobbled it in her effort to recover, she ended up stabbing herself instead.

"Ouch." Jessica pulled the needle free and looked at her fingertip, where a bright line of blood had already welled up. She sucked on her finger, then took a squeeze tube of wound gel from her kit and spurted a tiny bit of it over the laceration and the puncture. Her own immediate need resolved, Jessica put the medical supplies away and returned to the task at hand. She picked up the last item Zana had provided, the headphones. Dr. Acorns gently settled them over Tycho's ears before gathering up her tablet and tapping into a subset of one of the playlists she'd used on Potato. Granted, Tycho wouldn't benefit from seeing any of the images, but the soundtrack should also have been imprinted on the virus. If she was right, that might be enough to trigger the learned associations. Together with the adrenaline injection, it could kickstart the virus. The tablet confirmed that a sequence of several hours of war movies' audio tracks had successfully queued. Jessica hit play.

"I'm sorry, Tycho. This isn't good science. I'm basically grasping at straws and abandoning all protocols. And don't get me started on my Hippocratic oath. But what's the alternative? I don't have a lot of confidence that Mr. Cooper is going to be able to come through with anything, and if I sit here and do nothing, it's only a matter of time before the Box find us, realize we're both infected with versions of the virus, and kill us outright."

She fiddled with the vitals monitor the madam had provided, double-checked the sync with her tablet and that the data was pouring in and archiving for her later review, foolhardy as it might be to worry about there even being a 'later.'

"But if I'm correct... Well, it wouldn't be the first time desperation led to unorthodox breakthroughs. I may not be right, but attempting to spur your virus into action is at least a testable hypothesis. It's the best I can come up with, considering the resources I have access to. I'm guardedly optimistic, but given your brain damage, I don't want to make any promises. At this point, all we can do is pray it works. The good news is that if it doesn't, you'll never know." Jessica sighed and patted Tycho's hand, then stood and returned to pacing the room.

She instinctively raised her finger to suck on it again. But it was already healed. Her skin was perfectly smooth.

"Well, well. That's an interesting development."

The doctor looked over at Tycho and then back to her finger. Opening up a new data input, she directed the focus of her tablet and scanned her own vitals. Nothing had changed since the scan she'd performed shortly after arriving at the bordello. The unique markers of the virus allowed her to track its location in all three of its human hosts. Her version had continued to concentrate itself in the vicinity of her medulla. But that's all it had done. It hadn't disrupted her kidney function, nor had it activated to rewrite her DNA and erase the congenital disease that would take her life within the next two years. It could, though. All her simulations guaranteed it. The effects Mr. Cooper had experienced—eliminating his stage four cirrhosis, restoring his vacuum-damaged lungs, healing multiple breaks and fractures of his bones—were proof.

But not for her. Not yet. Except for repairing a laceration Mr. Cooper claimed he'd seen during their escape from the Box ranch and this new fix to her finger, the virus was still dormant in her. She tapped her tablet to record a note.

"Current evidence suggests the version of the virus in my system progresses in stages. After concentrating in proximity to my body's adrenaline production, it has demonstrated its ability to facilitate rapid—albeit superficial—healing. That's what I had wrong. It doesn't work all at once. Larger changes, like actually rewriting the host's cells, is its own separate stage, assuming that the virus can even be coaxed into entering that state."

Maybe that was it. Maybe the virus in her body just needed a push. Maybe.

The idea of what she was about to do sent quivers down her spine, but as soon as the thought occurred, she knew she had no choice but to follow through. They were out of time and options.

"I'm sorry, Tycho. Normally I would do one experiment at a time..." Using one hand and her teeth, she tied off her own arm with a length of tubing from the kit and found a promising vein. She filled a new syringe with epinephrine and, before she could change her mind, injected herself.

"Okay, now we wait and see. With luck, one of us will come out of this with a fully active virus and a new lease on life." She studied her tablet, watching as its readings reflected the adrenaline's effects. Her heart rate began rising. Her blood pressure likewise climbed as peripheral blood vessels clamped down. There was a surge of hyperglycemia and an accompanying bump in lactic acid, all typical responses.

Her hands spasmed and the tablet tumbled from her grasp to the floor alongside the bed. Without thinking, she bent to retrieve it. The world spun, her vision turned into an ever-narrowing gray tunnel, and a moment later she collapsed onto the bed alongside Tycho.

CHAPTER ELEVEN

The data center had seen better days, which is to say it was like most everything else Coop had experienced on Titan, with the notable exception of the facilities at the Box ranch. But it was all relative, and compared with the cramped quarters and vile odors of Hugo's, the data center with its spacious, private work cubicles and painfully bright lighting was like a walk on the beach in Aruba on a winter's morning. The endless array of inspirational posters plastered on every wall was a bit much, though.

The facility's lone employee proved considerably less surly than the bartender Coop had contended with earlier. She explained the process for accessing a terminal, took his payment for its use, then wandered away to give him privacy to view whatever had brought him in.

"We're quite the pair, aren't we?" Coop remarked.

«Yeah, Ben. We are. You forgot to have a life while you were busy pretending to be other people. And I am an amalgamation of roles yearning for a real existence.»

"I wonder which of us is the understudy."

Dyrk laughed inside Coop's head.

The screen came to life and Coop set to work. First, at Dyrk's insistence, he pulled up an article on computer network exploitation. Dyrk instructed him to keep his eyes on the screen and move through it as fast as possible.

Coop scrolled slowly.

«*Faster.*»

"I can't read it that fast."

«*You don't need to read it at all. I can read it as fast as it goes by on the screen.*»

Coop scrolled faster.

«*More.*»

Coop's fingers slapped at the machine's directional touchpad, pushing the data center's unit to the maximum until the textbook scrolled across the screen at warp speed before it bounced when he reached the end of the document.

"You get all that?"

«*Sure did.*»

"Seriously?"

«*I am a man with a particular set of skills, good buddy. Now, pull up everything you can find on Box technology.*»

An hour later, Coop had found and scrolled through five textbooks and a couple dozen scholarly articles on Box research and technology. It hadn't made any sense to him, just an unending blur of text and schematics, but Dyrk seemed satisfied. After each one, Dyrk provided Coop with increasingly arcane instructions for the next data search. It wasn't like Coop had a better idea, so he typed and swiped as instructed.

«*Eureka!*»

"What? What is it?"

«*I found what we need. Not all in one place, mind you, but by pulling the pieces together from all the materials we've reviewed. The hard part is done. That just leaves the tricky part.*»

"Tricky? Tricky how?"

«*Trust me, Ben. Just trust me. And, follow my instructions. Time for some very different data searches.*»

Coop complied with Dyrk's new set of search instructions and opened databases about Titan's residents. More accurately, their medical records, financial transactions, bank statements, and so on.

"Is this going to get us in trouble?" Coop wondered.

«No. Well, probably not. It might trigger some flags, but we should be fine if we hurry.»

"Again, not the answer I was hoping for. What are we looking for, anyway?"

«I don't know yet. But I will soon.»

"Huh?"

«I'm looking for patterns. When I find what we need, I'll know it. Right now, I'm just compiling the data, like I did with the material on the Box. I'm pulling the pieces together. It's like solving a jigsaw puzzle without knowing what it's supposed to look like until suddenly it does.»

Coop scrolled through one enormous database after another while Dyrk hummed the soundtrack from *Beverly Hills Cop* in his head.

Finally, midway through a database of public employees, Dyrk told him to double back. He hit reverse and scrolled slowly.

«Stop. That's him. That's our bitch.»

"Bitch? Where did that come from? Did Jess show Potato prison movies when you were being created?"

Dyrk said nothing, leaving Coop to stare at the screen and the profile image of a beefy, rough-looking man with eyes like an angry dog. He seemed vaguely familiar. "Why do I feel like I know this guy?"

«Because he's Officer Octavian Belzer, the cop you beat up in your cell when you started your incredibly epic prison escape. You crushed him. Remember? It was amazeballs. I wish they'd put that *footage on TV.»*

"He's the one you want to find? We beat him down and probably got him fired. Humiliated at a minimum. What good is he? That guy's going to hate us."

«You,» specified Dyrk. «*Without a doubt, he hates* you. *Not me. He doesn't know me. And I'm lovable. But his intense loathing for you doesn't matter because he doubtless hates the Box more than he hates you. It's a visceral thing, and he's been living with it a lot longer. You may not remember, but he said some pretty racist and xenophobic stuff about them. Most importantly for us, based on patterns of imports and exports that he really should have hidden better, I'm fairly certain he moonlights as a weapons dealer. Let's pay him a visit.*»

"Are you nuts? A weapons dealer? Why?"

«*Because he's going to give us the gear to take out the Box.*»

"Why would he do that? Did you forget about the part where he hates us? Sorry, me."

«*It's the ol' maxim of 'the enemy of my enemy,' Ben. We're going to show him how to take out the Box and maybe, just maybe, get rich doing it. Would you need more motivation than that?*»

"Hate and greed. That's a pretty intense combination," Coop agreed.

«*That's what I was thinking. You in?*»

Cooper nodded to himself. "Okay, it's worth a shot."

«*Great, but one more thing.*»

"Yeah?"

«*The whole 'get rich' part? We're going to keep that for ourselves.*»

CHAPTER TWELVE

Dyrk directed Coop to the spaceport's outer fringes, where lesser habitats and modules had begun life beyond the main dome before eventually being allowed to connect. In theory, everything there was up to code and perfectly safe. The viral echo had downloaded a plethora of maps and detailed directories of the environs during their time at the data center. He now used that knowledge to guide them with a local's skill through a maze of streets that were little more than collections of alleys with pressure-sealing gates at every end in case of a breach. Their destination was a sad little district full of mom-and-pop shops that looked more like converted storage sheds tacked on to the main street than commercial establishments.

Coop had spent the entire walk jumping at shadows, half expecting one of the Box to spot him and attack at any minute.

"I will never get used to this."

«Sure you will. A few more adventures like this and you'll be a grizzled veteran.»

"Okay. I *hope* I never get used to this."

«That's a terrible attitude. What if Rambo had said that after First

Blood? Where would civilization be? Worse off, that's where. Now, stop, Ben. We're here. The third store on the right.»

Coop tilted his head and pulled his hood back to look up at the hand-painted sign hanging over the shop's entrance.

Miss May's Family Entertainment

Coop was incredulous. "Our cop works out of a virtual reality game store?"

«His old lady owns the place. He runs his side business out of the back of the shop.»

"Okay. So, how are we going to play this?"

«We *aren't going to play anything. I am going to handle this. You just sit back and relax.»*

"Do you understand how impossible that is?"

«Not really, no. Now, move over.»

Coop did his best to relax as pressure built at the base of his skull. After a moment, and a very weird memory that was a cross between the smell of dry cleaning fluid and the view from the stage of his sixth-grade talent show, Coop's awareness of himself slid into the backseat of his own mind. He was a spectator again as Dyrk took control and marched his body into the arcade.

The inside of the establishment wasn't much better than the exterior. The entire structure was corrugated metal, as if it had been built from a Do-It-Yourself kit and then been abandoned because of missing pieces. Exposed cables ran over every wall and much of the floor and ceiling. Six virtual reality 'habitats' filled the shallow lobby of the store. They looked like vertical coffins.

Dyrk scanned the shop with Ben's eyes and spotted a black curtain pulled across a small alcove with an additional pair of VR habitats. Inwardly he felt Ben cringe.

Eww. I don't want to know what those are for. I just pray they have enough disinfectant. No. Forget I said that. There's no such thing as enough.

«*It takes all kinds to run the race,*» Dyrk told him.

Race? What race?

«*The human one.*»

One final habitat sat in the corner against the back wall with an out-of-order sign hanging from it. Unlike the other units, this one had been positioned flush with the wall. That, and the fact that there were no other obvious doors, suggested it was a not-so-hidden entrance into the backroom of Belzer's weapons business. Dyrk advanced to the shop's front counter but angled himself so he could keep one eye on the bogus VR unit. Behind the counter, a small troll of a woman spat tobacco juice into a plastic cup. She gave Dyrk the once over but couldn't be bothered to greet him.

«Hi there.»

She paused to spit again before speaking. "What can I do for you, sweetheart?"

From her tone and the spit, Dyrk did not get the sense the woman really cared about customer service.

«I'm looking for some…unique entertainment. I was told this was the place to come.»

"Were you now? Well, we've got all the latest in virtual reality." She gestured toward the habitats. "You want to be a hero, we've got it. You want to drive a starship, we can make it happen. If those don't do it for you—" She broke off and paused again, running her eyes up and down his frame, lingering strategically. "I've got a unit guaranteed to get your juices flowing, if you know what I mean."

Ugh. I need a shower.

The woman couldn't hear Coop's mental commentary, of course. She spit more tobacco juice into her cup. Dyrk sympathized with Coop, suspecting his host's juices might never flow again if he was forced to stay there much longer. Fortunately, that was when the door to the nonfunctioning VR coffin crashed open and Officer Octavian Belzer barreled out, red in the face. His fleshy jowls swung to and fro as he stormed across the room.

"You! You son of a bitch, I'm going to break your fucking head!"

The man lunged at Dyrk with all the finesse of a fat kid in a gym class dodgeball game. Even Coop, watching from the mental sidelines, would have been able to get out of the way. Dyrk didn't bother. Instead, he grabbed Belzer by both shoulders and redirected the momentum to spin him into the adjacent metal wall head first.

The entire structure shook from the impact, but Belzer recovered quickly. Apparently, a blow to the head wasn't the deterrent it would be to most sentient beings.

The weapons dealer rallied and lunged again. This time Dyrk stepped a bit to one side and stuck his foot out, and Belzer obligingly tripped and face-planted on the shop's bare floor. An instant later, Dyrk seated himself firmly on his former prison guard. He pulled the man's arms behind his back and pinned him.

«Now, now, Mr. Belzer. There is absolutely nothing to be gained by living in the past. Let's talk about the future. I have a proposition for you.»

"Fuck you."

Dyrk pulled one of the arms a bit higher, and Belzer screamed.

«Here are your options, Mr. Belzer. You can continue to resist me, in which case you're not going to leave me any choice but to break at least one of your arms. Or you can agree to hear me out, after which I let you go. What's your pleasure?»

The big man struggled vainly for a moment before sighing heavily.

"Whatever. Just get off me!"

«No problem. But when I do, before you try anything stupid,

remind yourself how easily I put you in this position and that next time I won't be nearly so gentle.»

Dyrk stood and backed away to allow Belzer the space to get to his feet. The weapons dealer took a minute to brush himself off and collect his bruised dignity. Coop noticed the woman behind the counter smirking.

"What do you want from me?"

«Mr. Belzer, you may not want to believe this, but we have a common interest.»

"Oh yeah. What's that?"

«We both hate the Box and would like to see them gone, not just from Titan but from our entire solar system. Sure, we have different reasons, but we both want the same result.»

Belzer's eyes almost crossed as he digested Dyrk's statement.

"Why should I believe you?"

«I can offer you information that is fatal to the Box avatar technology. No one else has this intel, and by sharing it I'm putting all of the Box at risk.»

"Okay. Tell me about it."

«There is a fatal flaw in the design of all the Box extensions. It exists in the shielding for one of the critical components. A weapon such as, say, a police stun baton, could be modified to burn out that component with a single touch to the right spot on their bodies. This will shut down the unit and render it useless until major repairs can be made.»

Belzer's beady eyes locked onto Dyrk like a hungry wolf staring at a chicken coop. "What spot do I have to hit?"

«Not so fast. I'll tell you that, but only in exchange for what I need.»

"And what's that?"

«I'll show you how to modify the batons, and in return I want you to produce several for my use. You have the experience and the tools, and I have the details. When you've provided me with the modified batons, you'll be able to make more for yourself and I'll have told you where to hit any Box to bring it down.»

The big man nodded, fueled by hatred for the Box. "All right. I'll help you. For Molly and Jeth."

Who are Molly and Jeth?

«*We don't know and don't need to know,*» Dyrk murmured in Coop's head. «*What's important to us is that Belzer's highly motivated to get back at the Box, and that means he'll give us what we need.*»

Visibly seething, Belzer beckoned to Dyrk. "Follow me."

He led the way through the bogus VR coffin and into the backroom, which was a workshop as well as a storage area. If the stenciling on the boxes could be believed, the room's shelves contained dozens of weapons and thousands of rounds of ammo, not just stun gear and fluid guns, but the kind of ballistic weapons that were outlawed in domed cities and habitat modules throughout the solar system. A plastic workbench ran the length of the other wall. It was covered with a full range of tools and equipment for modifying existing weapons to enhance their firepower or remove the manufacturer's safety features. A scattering of cheap folding tables bore endless parts.

From his mental backseat, Coop let out an imaginary whistle. *For a prison guard, our boy Belzer looks to be one hell of an entrepreneur.*

Belzer strode to one of the shelves and opened a case. A moment later he turned and deposited four stun batons on the workbench.

"These are fully charged. Now, what needs to be changed?"

Dyrk glanced at the workbench and located a disposable tablet. Using his index finger as a stylus, he jotted down the specific voltage pattern from his research before handing over the device.

Belzer scowled. "That's it?"

«I know, right? Seems too easy to be true. Which may be why

no one ever thought to try it before now. You can handle the modifications, right?»

Another scowl. "Sure. Now get out of my way and let me work." He pulled a chair up to his workbench and briefly picked up each baton in turn, disengaging their power sources and setting them back down. He deftly opened up the first baton and began applying hair-fine tools to the device's innards.

Forget what I said before. He's one hell of a weapons smith! Talk about wasted talent.

Belzer's hands practically flew as he tweaked, tested, and re-tweaked the baton over and over until he was satisfied. He plugged one end of a different tool into the baton's charging port and the other end into a diagnostic tablet. A string of script flowed across the screen. Coop couldn't decipher any of it, but whatever it was, Dyrk liked the results. He nodded and Belzer unplugged the baton, sealed it up, and moved on to the next one.

Most of an hour passed before Belzer set his tools down with a grunt. "Finished." He gathered the four modified stun batons and placed them in front of Dyrk.

"These match your specs. Now tell me what I need to know."

Dyrk nodded and pointed to a spot on the man's left hip just above his butt cheek. «Right here. The shielding is compromised at this joint on each of the different models. Hit it with the baton and you'll fry a critical modulator that will signal an immediate shutdown.»

Belzer grinned and scooped up all four batons, then stuffed them into a black backpack. "Nice doing business with you."

Dyrk accepted the pack without a word and left the shop.

CHAPTER THIRTEEN

Out on the street, Dyrk relinquished control in mid-step as he started them back the way they'd come.

"Dyrk, was that really a good idea? You just gave a xenophobic, racist asshole the ability to bring down another race."

«*No. I gave him the knowledge of how to do it. He doesn't have anything close to the ability to pull it off. Maybe. Maybe, he can take down one of them. But seriously, Ben, I doubt he could manage even that much. Even if he does, the others will get him. He's not fast enough or smart enough. Hence, he's not capable of bringing down all of them. He is dumb enough to try though, which will bring its own rewards.*»

"Okay. How is that going to be any different for us?"

«*That's easy,*» Dyrk assured Coop. «*The difference is, we're going to shut down* all *the extensions, one after another.*»

"So...this is all part of some plan?"

«*Oh, absolutely! Keep an eye out for a public comm terminal, and we'll move on to stage two.*»

Moments later, Coop spotted an advertising kiosk with graffiti-proof screens offering the latest and greatest entertainments and bargains on Titan. Squeezed in among the announcements for genuine imitation Kobe beef and anti-gravity rumpus rooms renting by the half-hour lay a pair of public comm terminals. Coop was about to press his thumb to one of the terminals for access when Dyrk froze the offending hand like a grandmother with a rigged cookie jar, and slid back into control of their shared body.

«Hold on. The whole point of using public comms is so you don't log in. Watch and learn.»

Dyrk pressed the strap of the backpack they'd gotten from Belzer to the comms activation emblem and then lifted it higher to block the camera. «Collect call to Scatola, Box Ranch, Habitat Module One.»

Are you insane? Coop demanded.

«Shhh! I've got this.»

Fractals danced on the screen while the terminal waited for a connection.

He'll trace the call.

Dyrk tried to calm Coop. «Trust me, he won't. I'll give him something else to focus on. And even if he did, it wouldn't matter. We'll be long gone before the Box can react.»

You can't know that. Hang up now, before it's too late—

The fractals dissolved into the face of the avatar of Scatola that had traveled to Earth to recruit Coop. He tapped something on his side and frowned when the picture didn't improve.

"Who is this? What do you want? This had better be important," Scatola demanded in his nasally British accent.

Dyrk dropped his voice an octave and stretched out his vowels, sounding nothing like Ben Cooper. «I have information you want. About your missing doctor and the old drunk she's carting around. For the right price, I know where they are.»

"Really. I don't have time for games. Tell me."

«They are hiding out, using two locations. They plan to move out of hiding soon and then dart back and forth on a random schedule between them to avoid staying still for too long. You'll have to watch both locations if you hope to find them.»

Scatola scoffed. "That won't be a problem. Where are the two locations?"

Dyrk ignored the question. «Yeah, you say that, but what you don't know is, they've hired themselves some muscle. That's how I learned all this.»

"You've only just entered into their employ, and you're already betraying them? How very human." Scatola didn't even try to hide his contempt.

«It's not like that,» explained Dyrk. «They're not making sense. They said they won't be taken, no matter what. Which means if you come in hot and heavy, me and the others they've hired are going to take the worst of it. And we'll likely lose anyway. This isn't a betrayal. It's, um, pre-emptive negotiations.»

"I understand. Now, tell me where they are."

«Not so fast, Mr. Box man. I'm probably forfeiting my payment from them, and I've gotta make a living, same as anyone else. If you want the location, you need to deposit half my fee up-front. The rest will be due upon you successfully locating them."

Scatola fell silent.

You oversold it, Coop despaired. *He's not buying it.*

Before Dyrk could respond, the Box was speaking again and nodding. "Very well. What is your fee?"

Dyrk provided the alien with an insultingly large number and the information for the bank account he had set up earlier. At the same time, he used the adjacent terminal to access that new account and kept hitting the refresh key until the account balance included Scatola's deposit. Once it had, Dyrk rattled off a pair of GPS coordinates.

«That's both locations, Mr. Box man. They should be making a move to one or the other within two hours' time. Good hunting.»

The Box logged off without bothering to reply.

Dyrk closed both comm screens and dropped back, letting Coop take control again.

"Where did you send them?"

«I'll tell you in a minute. But first we need to move on to stage three, and quickly.»

"What and where is stage three?"

«A pawn shop,» answered Dyrk. *«Walk straight and turn right at the third intersection. It will be a few doors down on your left.»*

"You know where the spaceport's pawnshop is?"

«No, I know where all five of the spaceport's pawnshops are. I've got a map of the entire place in my head, remember? And it includes the name and address of every commercial property. That pawnshop happens to be the nearest and the one that best suits our needs. But we're on the clock now, so hurry.»

Coop hurried ahead two blocks before hanging a right. On the left, just past a convenience shop and a laundromat, was the promised pawnshop. The door was open and he walked right in. Somewhere ahead of him, a buzzer sounded.

Pawnshops, at least human ones, are pretty much the same anywhere you go. Only the smells are different, and those reflect the preferred cuisine of whoever is running the place. Coop detected the heavy scent of curry, redolent with turmeric and cumin. In addition to the aroma, the shop was jammed with merchandise. Every inch of space had been crammed to bursting by some piece of junk or another. Electronics. Artwork. Games. Sex toys. Everything you never knew you wanted or needed was apparently for sale.

«People buy used sex toys?»

"Ah, yes. Dyrk, let me teach you an important lesson about being human. There are some questions you don't want answered. Now, what are we doing here?"

«We need comms, and we need a place to fence the Box tech when we get our hands on it.»

"Fence?"

«Oh yeah. We're gonna need money and we'll need it fast.»

"The guy has banjos and vibrators on the wall. You really think he moves black-market alien hardware?"

«I'm certain. I checked his accounts, and he moves a lot of cash around. Big sums of money that clearly have nothing to do with the junk you see on display here. This is just a cover.»

The owner, a small human of mixed descent, wandered out from a back room. He pushed aside a curtain of neon-hued plastic beads, and his big eyes focused on Coop.

"Hello, my friend. I am Patel. How may I help you?"

Dyrk sounded off in Coop's head. *«Okay, let me show you how this is done. We're going to tag team this guy. Ready?»*

Without waiting for a reply, Dyrk shoved Coop's consciousness to the side.

«Howdy, Patel. I need a couple of comms devices. Anonymous comms devices. And I may also have some stuff to sell soon. I wanted to see if we could come to an arrangement.»

The small man bobbed his head and stroked his white goatee.

"Okay, my friend. One thing at a time. You want comms. I got comms."

What the hell? Coop muttered internally as he pushed Dyrk into the mental backseat.

Oblivious to the conflict going on inside his customer's brain case, Patel walked down the counter and rummaged through a large plastic container on the floor. He emerged with a pair of antiquated but serviceable communication pads.

"These are what you want. You can search for data and make voice and video calls. You can pay for the service in advance with credit chips. All very discreet and untraceable once you end your call."

"I'll take them," Coop responded before setting some of his last physical currency on the counter.

The small man scooped up the credits without offering either a price or change. He turned his beady eyes up to his customer's face. "Now, you said you may have some items to sell."

Realizing he had no idea what Dyrk had been planning, Coop relaxed and let the action hero take control once more.

«Yes, sir. It is rare technology. The type of stuff biomedical researchers might want to get their hands on.»

"Hmmm. As you can see, I run a pawn shop, not a clearing house for rare technology."

«Yeah, you say that. But the data says otherwise. Listen. In the very near future, I will have access to some proprietary Box hardware. You want it.»

"I see. Can you be...more specific? Precisely what kind of Box hardware?"

Yeah, what kind of hardware?

«Box extensions. The very bodies they use to house their consciousness when they walk around among us. Not the sort of thing that's been available to humans. Ever. An enterprising technologist could go far studying them, taking them apart, figuring out what makes them tick. If Elon Musk is still alive, give him a call. He'll love this stuff.»

The pawn broker looked unconvinced. "The engineering specifications for such things are readily available. I don't see the value."

«Those specs contain only general descriptions of several sealed components, without details for composition or construction. The actual bits themselves have never been in the hands of human beings before. They'd be potentially priceless to a talented engineer.»

Patel shrugged. "I don't know who this person you describe might be. I am a simple pawnshop owner. But, perhaps I can find a buyer who might want it for scrap. I'm probably losing money, but I can offer you ten creds per hundred kilograms."

Dyrk rolled his eyes and shook his head. «Do I look like a fool, Patel? Fine, if that's how you want to play it, I'll just bring my offer over to Hassan on the other side of the spaceport. I'm sure he'll see the value of what I'm bringing and make me a legitimate offer for each Box extension.»

The man's eyes flitted back and forth nervously. "Okay, okay. Slow your roll, my friend. Sheesh. I will offer you twenty thousand creds per extension. No pawn. Just cash sale."

«Nope. Five hundred thousand creds.»

The man cringed and feigned being stabbed in the heart. "My special friend, no. I'm speculating here. I'd still have to find a buyer. This is surely a mistake, but... I could go as high as one hundred thousand creds for each."

«Patel, a man like you has a contacts list with multiple buyers. You'll either start a bidding war among them or sell to more than one. Four hundred thousand creds for each Box extension I can make available to you.»

"That's impossible. You would be taking food from my six children and my ailing wife. Please, two hundred thousand creds."

«Three hundred, Patel. And that's my final offer.»

"Let us compromise. Two hundred fifty thousand."

«When I said 'final offer,' I meant it.» Dyrk turned to go.

"Wait! Wait! You're killing me, my friend, but... I sense a great destiny in you. I will agree to three hundred."

Dyrk turned back and offered Patel his hand. «Done. Make sure you have the money ready. I'll expect you to transfer it to my account as soon as you pick up the goods.»

"What? Me pick them up? Oh, no, my friend. Surely for three hundred thousand creds per unit, you'll be delivering them."

«That would require me to know where your warehouse is,» Dyrk observed. «Both the public one and the second warehouse that even your wife doesn't know about.»

"How do you—"

Dyrk brought a finger to the man's lips, shushing him. «Let's just say that tracking the routes of goods and services here on Titan is a hobby of mine. Expect a call from me soon.»

With a mental whiff of weariness, Dyrk surrendered control of their shared body.

«You're on. Dramatic exit, if you please.»

Coop tossed his head back and looked down his nose at the pawnbroker. He spun on his heel and strode from the store. On the off chance the little man had followed him out and was still watching, Coop marched ramrod straight down the street and around the corner.

"How did you know that would work?"

«Two things. First, he has written out loan slips to every guy with a record for theft in this planetary system. That means he's a fence. Second, the leasing records I scanned earlier show two warehouses owned by him, one under his name and another under an alias that eventually tracks back to him if you can step back far enough to see the big picture. And third, according to marriage records, Hassan is his wife's brother and there's a record of the police being called in to break up petty disputes between them going back years. No way was he going to let a large score go to that guy.»

Coop laughed out loud. "Dyrk, you may understand more about human relationships than you give yourself credit for."

CHAPTER FOURTEEN

Jessica woke up with a pounding skull. Her hands clutched at the back of her head, and as her arms moved across cool sheets she realized she was lying facedown on a bed. "Unnh. Not what I expected. Why would adrenaline knock me out? That makes no sense. If anything, it should have had the opposite effect."

She stood carefully, attentive to any signals her body might send as she gently stretched. No alarms sounded, and neither muscles nor bones ached. Aside from the headache, she felt pretty good. For reasons still to be determined, she'd apparently fallen down on the bed next to Tycho when the injection had taken hold. The comatose girl seemed fine. Jessica snatched up her tablet and accessed the diagnostic software she'd installed. Tycho showed no effect from her own injection. Jessica was about to set the tablet aside when she saw a message waiting for her.

From: 2nd Titanian Trust and Investment Corporation
To: Acct# 8771614389494
A deposit was recently made to your account. If you

believe this transaction was made in error, please notify us immediately. Thank you for your business.

She tapped the link to view the transaction, almost dropping the tablet when she saw a balance of nearly three million Titanian creds. "Wow. Well, at least something went according to plan. I have to admit Mr. Cooper is getting the job done, Tycho. And then some. That's more than enough money to get us back to Earth. In fact…there's plenty left over to explore an idea I just had."

Jessica patted Tycho's foot as she exited the room and carefully closed and locked the door behind herself.

Dr. Acorns descended the steps to the bordello's parlor and found Madam Zana seated among half a dozen of the women she employed. They were watching some incomprehensible xenodrama on the wall screen. It didn't matter.

"Madam Zana?"

"Yes, dear?" the alien asked without taking her eyes off the screen.

"I need to find a man."

"Sorry honey, that ain't my line of business. I've got lots of girls though, if you're feeling adventurous. No judgment here."

Jessica's mouth hung open for a moment. She recovered. "No. Sorry, I should have been clearer. The person I'm seeking doesn't have to be male. He, or she, must possess particular training."

Madam Zana turned from the screen, which must have been a signal to the women around her. They slipped away, languidly moving across the parlor to land on other bits of furniture, their attention overtly focused away. Only when the last of them had settled did Zana turn her gaze to Jessica. "I'm listening."

"I need an electrical engineer. Or a really skilled electrician. One that can keep his mouth shut."

The Cormyrian nodded. "I may have just the guy. He's a client. So, if you and I come to an agreement, I'll handle paying him and making sure he keeps his mouth shut. I assume we're talking Titanian credits? How does fifty thousand sound?"

"Terrifying and slightly nauseating," Jessica admitted, then added, "But, um, no judgment."

Madam Zana raised one delicate eyebrow and tapped one hoof.

"Right. Um, I mean... Under the circumstances, that's totally acceptable. Thank you."

"I'll make the call."

CHAPTER FIFTEEN

Dyrk guided them in a zigzag across the spaceport. They paused at a half-dozen bank machines along the way to withdraw modest sums of cash from the funds he'd extorted from Scatola. They'd left the tunnels and poorer areas behind and climbed to the surface level, though they were still far from the hustle and bustle of vehicles coming and going at the center of the spaceport. They passed a blend of high-end low-altitude office buildings, some really nice restaurants, even an art gallery.

From the back of his own head, Coop asked, *I thought the plan was to disable Box extensions and call Patel in to haul them away? What do we need cash for anyway? And why not grab it all from one place?*

«Ben, it's a pretty safe bet that the Box will be on our trail soon. Given his resources, I'm guessing it's fifty-fifty that Scatola tagged the payment before he transferred it to our account. We know he's not looking to leave any loose ends, so if he knows the account, he'll know when and where it's been accessed, and swoop in on us. To confound that, I'm leaving a trail that wanders all over.»

That sounds like an argument not to tap the account at all, Coop pointed out

«Maybe, but we need to give him time to get to the locations we told him about, so we need to kill a little time. And if we don't get cash, how will we go shopping?»

As if to make his point, Dyrk took a sharp turn and walked into a clothing store.

«We're about to go to war, Ben. I thought we could spare the time and creds to dress the part. Look around and let me know if you see anything you really like. Or really hate, for that matter.»

Coop found himself in control of their shared body. He shrugged and started up the nearest aisle of menswear.

"If we're going to war, wouldn't we be better served buying some body armor? Or one of those impact polymer suits that stiffen when struck so they can stop bullets?"

«What? Are you kidding me? Heck, no! You know what the problem with body armor like that is?»

"It keeps you alive?"

«It tells everyone around you that you're wearing body armor!»

"And that's a problem because..."

«Because if they know you're armored up, they'll upgrade their weapons beyond the specs of your armor, which defeats the point.»

"Well, okay, maybe, but only if they have access to that kind of hardware."

«Which the Box do. No, far better for us to wear something comfortable but durable. A breathable pico-fiber with a tight enough weave to turn a knife, but that says 'Hey, shoot me in the chest.'»

"Yeah, but what happens if someone shoots us in the chest anyway?"

«Not to worry. Short of getting shot in the head, I can heal anything that happens to us. And I'm pretty sure I could handle a head-shot too.»

"I'm going to suggest we not put that one to the test, okay?"

«Deal. Now, what do you think of that suit in front of us?»

"Are you kidding? That's crap. Most of this stuff is third-rate. Trust me, Dyrk, I know how to wear clothes. If you're serious about this, then let's do it right. I used to fly to Beijing and Tuscany for bespoke suits."

«That's the good stuff?»

"Nothing finer. But we're a long way from either, so don't get your hopes up. Since we're short on time, we're going to have to buy off the rack."

Half an hour later, Coop emerged from the shop in possibly the third most expensive suit on Titan. It wasn't all that high of a bar, but still. He looked more respectable than he had in a long while. More importantly, the change of clothes did wonders for his morale. He strutted along the avenue in the swankiest section of the habitat, feeling better than he had in years. The suit didn't owe him a penny.

«Feeling good?»

"Actually, I am. Thanks."

«Glad you're happy. Because very soon, all sorts of things are going to start happening very quickly. See the restaurant up ahead on the right? That's our first stop.»

Coop strode to the entrance like he owned the place. Like Ben Cooper exiting a limo and stepping onto the red carpet at a movie premiere. "The place looks posh."

He stepped inside, and for the first time, he felt like he was back on Earth. Back in L.A. even. In his element. "Posh" didn't begin to cover it.

"Nice place," Coop commented appreciatively. "I like the big open kitchen in the center of the dining area. It's always good to see where your food is being prepared."

«I'll take your word for it. Now, get us a seat. I'll take over when it's show time, but for now, conserving my strength is key.»

Coop sighed. "Just so you know, this isn't easy for me."

«Why not?»

"Well, for over sixty years, I've been the only person in control of my body."

«Yeah, and just look what you did with it.»

The actor winced. "That isn't relevant."

«Why not?»

"Because I said it's not. And just listen. We humans get kind of attached to our bodies. They are a big part of our identity. They are literally how we identify each other."

«If you like them so much, why do you poison and abuse them all the time?»

"Stop confusing this with facts. I'm just saying you could show a little more sensitivity, is all."

«Okay, Ben. Sorry about that. But I won't always have time to make you feel good about things. Sometimes, action is required.»

"I've got it. I'm getting used to this. Just work with me. Now, let me get us a table. I'm assuming you want a view of the front door?"

«Yeah. Something along the back wall if you can.»

Coop deftly palmed a sizable donation to the maître d, who showed him to a booth lined with real leather—a luxury that meant a lot more on Titan than on Earth.

A young woman brought him water, and Dyrk slid into control of Coop's body to wait. It didn't take long.

Nine extensions of the Box entered the restaurant like a gang of pretentious thugs. Six of them had the smug, human-like bearing of Scatola, and three appeared to be extensions of Pudełko, with his much more utilitarian and robotic model.

The extensions ignored the greeter and fanned out around the restaurant. The chef and his brigade in the center of the establishment continued their work, but the other diners, both human and the handful of xenons present, noted the rude robots and their overt display of aggression.

«Good.» Dyrk grinned. *«Scatola shared our news with his fellows. That will make this easier.»* Dyrk kept his head down and waited. One of Scatola's extensions was making his way through the tables nearby, checking the diners one at a time. When the young lady who had brought the water passed between Dyrk and the

Box, the action hero made his move. Using her as a screen, Dyrk slipped out of the booth and closed the distance to the first Box.

The viral echo held a stun baton behind his leg as he approached Scatola. He was no longer trying to hide, and he took full advantage of the extension's surprise as the Box looked up and saw Coop coming toward him.

The Box drew itself up but didn't move his feet.

In one smooth motion, Dyrk leapt forward and stabbed out precisely at the avatar's side with the baton. A jolt of electricity slammed into the Box. Scatola jerked twice and fell loudly to the floor, where he collapsed, motionless and deactivated.

«*It worked! One down, eight to go.*» Dyrk cheered in Coop's head.

Why do you sound surprised? Wasn't this part supposed to be foolproof? I thought this was just part of the plan.

«*No plan survives contact with the enemy,*» Dyrk quoted as he looked to his left and right. He found his next target near the counter surrounding the open kitchen. It was one of Pudełko's models, and it had leaned over the counter as it tried to look underneath all the tables inside the food preparation area. The extension presented a very tempting target.

Dyrk stepped onto a chair and used it to leap over the nearest table. He landed on both feet and quickly advanced on the robot. He had the baton already extended in his hand when one of the Scatolas cried out a warning.

"Pudełko, behind you!"

Pudełko stood up to leverage itself off the counter, but it was too late. Before it could turn, Dyrk was on it, ramming the stun baton against its backside and watching the avatar thrash about. Its multiple arms and appendages clanked into its carapace and smacked against the faux-wood divider before it collapsed to its knees, its metal body leaning against the waist-high wall.

«*Two! Ha ha!*»

Oh, dear lord. Coop thought. *This must be what it's like when people teach their kids to drive, and all they can do is brace themselves and close their eyes.*

Box extensions closed in from all over the restaurant. Coop very badly wanted to close his eyes, but Dyrk seemed to be in fine spirits as he ran up the back of the prone Pudełko avatar and jumped into the kitchen, landing on one of the metal prep tables.

Customers began screaming and yelling. Some stayed where they stood, and others ran for the door. Chairs tumbled over and general pandemonium ensued.

«*This is glorious!*» Dyrk crowed.

Dyrk reached down and grabbed a handful of uncooked rice, then sprinted down the length of the table. Coop's hijacked feet danced between plates and cooking utensils as he went. Amazingly, he never missed a step.

Straight ahead, a Scatola bounded over the divider and landed inside the kitchen area. He climbed up on the table and raced toward Dyrk, who continued his charge.

What are you doing? Coop demanded.

When Dyrk was just meters away from the oncoming Box, he whipped his hand out and let the rice fly straight at Scatola's face. The Box's sensors immediately tried to analyze the threat, devoting most of its sensory processing to tracking hundreds of individual grains of rice. It was too much, and the Box pulled up short for the second it took to sort through the incoming data. That was all Dyrk needed.

He slid to Coop's knees and stabbed the baton into Scatola's hip. The avatar spasmed and fell over, landing on top of a grill. The Box's synthetic face immediately began to sizzle. The smell of burning polymer filled the air along with the sound of cursing cooks.

«I'm smokin'! Wait, *you* are. Striiiike three!» Dyrk crowed at the charring avatar.

Dyrk scanned the restaurant and found the nearest threat. Another Scatola had pushed through the panicked diners and angry staff to reach the kitchen area. This one did not jump over the wall, but rather took his time opening the pair of swinging dividers that led into the open kitchen.

Dyrk bent down and grabbed a basket of dinner rolls. They smelled delicious, so he popped one in his mouth, holding the glorious, buttery carbs between his teeth while he flung the remaining rolls at this new enemy's face. It didn't have quite the same effect as the rice, but it did buy him a second or two as the avatar batted the rolls out of the air with astonishing speed.

«Nice moves,» Dyrk noted as he closed in on the avatar.

Scatola didn't bother with a reply. He swung a fist at Dyrk's head, which the action hero effortlessly blocked. In response, Dyrk aimed the baton in a series of strikes at Scatola's face. The Box parried them with his arms one after another, but Dyrk's intention wasn't to damage his opponent. He was using the failed strikes to maneuver the avatar against the table.

When Dyrk had Scatola in place, he swung out his left hand and let the Box smack it away easily. The move left the Box wide open, and the table kept him from backing away. Dyrk jammed the stun baton into Scatola's side and watched him crash to the floor.

«Damn, I'm—» Dyrk squealed as he was lifted from behind.

One of the Pudełkos had snuck up on him in the midst of his gloating. It had its robotic arms wrapped around Coop and had begun squeezing his torso in its vice-like limbs.

«Not... good,» Dyrk gasped.

Do something! Coop mentally shouted.

Dyrk shifted left and right, trying to shake free, but Pudełko held him tight. So, he threw his hands up and slipped straight down from the robot's grasp.

«Haha! Child's play.»

That was when Pudełko slammed a metal fist down against his head, which sent Dyrk to the floor.

What are you doing with my body? Get up! Coop fumed.

Dyrk rolled to the side and got out of Pudełko's reach. As he rose onto a knee, he saw Pudełko's torso spin to face him. It was the perfect opportunity and Dyrk did not miss it.

He jumped to his feet and swept his left arm out, gathering a mass of salad ingredients in his wake. He flung them at Pudełko in a rainbow of fiber and vitamins. The peppers, spinach, and tomatoes covered Pudełko's face and sensors, causing it to throw its four arms up to pick away the vegetarian debris. While it was doing this, Dyrk strolled over and tapped the baton against the Box's side. The robot crashed and died with salad all over its face.

«You've got something in your teeth,» Dyrk jeered at the avatar.

Coop groaned internally. *That was terrible. Who uses lines like that? I know they're vintage classics, but you need to let go of those ancient Schwarzenegger movies!*

Dyrk's finely tuned and wholly artificial instincts told him he needed to move, so he jumped back onto the table and flung himself over the divider and into the dining area. He landed like a cat, crouched and ready to pounce.

A pair of Scatolas ran at Dyrk, one from either side. Dyrk grabbed the back of a wooden chair, and a wiry man who looked like a manager shouted, "Please, not the wood furniture! It's—" Dyrk spun and used his momentum to hurl the chair into one of the charging avatars. It slammed into his face and splintered, and the Scatola careened sideways into the kitchen counter. "...really expensive," the manager finished in a whimper.

Dyrk dismissed the manager's concern with a wink and swooped over to grab a bowl of soup. He flung it in the face of the other approaching Scatola without breaking stride, then slipped sideways one step out of the way to tuck and roll between two tables. The two blinded Scatolas crashed into one another and fell to the floor. Dyrk popped back up and needed only a moment to shock both out of commission.

Well played, Dyrk. Well played, Coop congratulated his partner.

The viral echo smiled to himself and his invisible audience, turning in a slow circle to regard the smattering of lingering diners, onlooking kitchen staff, and his last two opponents. The remaining Scatola and Pudełko extensions stood together about ten feet away. Clearly, they had decided to take a more cautious and measured approach.

"Mr. Cooper," the Scatola began. "It is time for this foolishness to end. You are in violation of your contract and must come with us. I promise you will not be harmed."

Coop was incredulous. *Does that asshole think I believe him?*

«*Seriously. Not to worry, I've got this,*» Dyrk responded silently in their shared mindspace.

Dyrk let his left hand rest gently on the table next to him and held the baton in his right fist. A red warning light on the weapon blinked, indicating it was almost out of power.

«Scatola, I only have two words for you and your lies. It's critically important that you understand them, because they represent the future of your interactions with humans from this day forward. Please listen carefully. Ready? Here it is: Eat me!» With that, Dyrk snatched a medium-rare steak from an abandoned table and flung it at the pompous avatar. The instant the meat had left his hand, Dyrk charged. Unfortunately, this Scatola wasn't thrown off by the beefy projectile. It merely tilted its head to the side and allowed the porterhouse to fly by.

Seeing the entrée fail to have an impact, Dyrk reversed course. Literally. He returned to a previously successful tactic, grabbing a tureen full of soup and casting an arc of cream-of-broccoli slime at the faces of his opponents.

The soup splattered all over the two avatars and their sensors. Scatola wiped furiously at his visual inputs and tried to backpedal out of the way. In doing so he collided with the appendages of the now confused Pudełko, and the pair became entangled.

Dyrk used the confusion to sidle up beside Scatola. «Try and think of it this way, Scatola. I am your God. Your sacrifice is appreciated.»

He jabbed the baton home, then shoved the deactivating Scatola onto Pudełko, who had just untangled itself and now toppled over again. Dyrk dispatched this last Pudełko while it struggled with the dead weight of its comrade. The pair of extensions fell to the restaurant floor in a heap of metallic and synthetic material.

«I told you this would be easy.» Dyrk gloated.

Are you trying to tell me you planned all of this?

«Not the specifics, no. But improvisation in the field and making the best of the materials at hand, that's one of the things I do best.»

Oh, please.

Dyrk just shrugged. «My results speak for themselves.» He knelt next to the lifeless machine and took the recently purchased comm unit from his backpack to contact the pawnbroker.

«Patel? This is your favorite provider of Box merchandise. I have nine units waiting for you here at the Tartarus restaurant in the spaceport's purple district. No, stop pretending you don't know where it is. Your own credit records show that you dined here last week. Never mind how I know. Just get over here and claim the merchandise. I'll expect to see two million seven hundred thousand Titanian creds showing up in my account. And move quickly. You wouldn't want someone realizing the value of the goods here and scooping them up because you dawdled. No, I can't stick around until you arrive. I need to move on to the next location and secure a few more for you. Expect another call within the hour.» Dyrk left the circuit open and tucked the comm unit underneath the prone Pudełko.

What's to keep him from just claiming the extensions and not making payment? Coop asked.

«Greed,» answered Dyrk. «That's why I mentioned there's

more coming. He'll pay for these, if only so he gets the chance to stiff us on the others and to ensure we don't sell them to his competition.»

He wants a monopoly so he can charge more.

«Bingo. Ready to do this all over again?»

Lead on.

Dyrk rose to his feet and looked around the restaurant. He took the time to establish eye contact with each of the remaining customers and staff in turn. «Dinner and a show, people. Dinner and a show. Please remember to tip your waiters. I'm out.» Dyrk held out the depleted stun baton and dropped it like a microphone. Nobody said a word to him, let alone tried to stop him, as he exited the building.

CHAPTER SIXTEEN

Jessica was engrossed in the data on her tablet when a knock sounded at the door. She practically jumped out of her skin. Again. "Dammit!"

She shook off the jitters and crossed to the door. "Yes? Who's there?"

"Madam Zana. The man you asked for is here with me."

"Oh, yeah," replied a man's voice from the other side.

"Shut up, Doug." This was Zana.

Just what I need.

Jessica opened the door and found Madam Zana crammed in the hallway with a bearded, heavyset man in coveralls. Predictably, his name tag read "Doug."

Doug looked Jessica up and down, grinning lasciviously. "How may I service you?"

"Eww. First, knock it off. Just try to not be such a...man for a few minutes. Please."

Doug looked crestfallen.

Idiot.

"Doug, do you have any experience with biologic propagation systems?"

"Sure. I've installed and configured basic ones at the clinic here. That's the easy part. But I'm not an expert. The hard part is getting the software. Do you have it?"

"I do. On my tablet. But I don't have any of the hardware."

"That's not a problem. Those units are all pretty modular and scale up from a common core. I should have a lot of the stuff I need down on my cart. And the rest I can get pretty quick from the medical supply shop. What's it for?"

"A patient of mine. That's all you need to know."

"Um..."

Jessica turned to Madam Zana. "You said he could be trusted."

"Oh, he can be. Unless he wants his wife to find out about where all his overtime money goes."

Doug looked at the floor, somehow having gone from a perv to a petulant child in the span of a minute. "So. When do I start?"

Jessica crossed her arms and nodded. "Right away. Get whatever relevant gear you have and then come back up here."

Madam Zana gave the doctor a curt nod. "Come find me if you require any additional assistance." She escorted Doug back out into the hall.

He wasn't gone for more than a few minutes before he returned with a duffel bag and a toolbox. His demeanor was that of a perfect gentleman, leaving Jessica wondering what Zana had said to him on the way down. Not that any of it mattered, so long as he could do the job.

Jessica explained what she needed and Doug, to his credit, didn't flinch at any of the technical vocabulary. When she'd finished, he followed up with a couple questions to confirm he'd understood the trickier parts and then immediately set to work. To her relief, Doug's earlier assessment was spot on. It made sense. Hardware on Titan was at a premium, and it had quickly become standard to build nearly everything using common components. Doug finished quickly, creating the diagnostic interface she needed. He mounted the resulting hardware in a black box that might have been a picnic basket in another life. She checked the connection with her tablet and set the apparatus on the bedside table. Data began to flow within seconds.

"Good job, Doug."

Doug's eyes lit up, hope springing eternal.

"No, Doug. Goodbye."

The creepy engineer shuffled out but paused before closing the door. "Are you sure there's nothing else you need?"

Jessica stopped herself from rolling her eyes as a possibility occurred to her.

"Actually… Do you know your blood type, Doug?"

"My blood type?"

She nodded. "I'm A positive, as is my patient. If you're a match, how would you feel about donating a pint?"

Doug shook his head. "I think I'm B. I don't recall if it's positive or negative or what, but I know it's B."

Jessica shrugged. "Well, it was just a thought. That's it then, thank you for your help."

She locked the door behind him and turned to Tycho. "You may not know it Tycho, but you just might save my life. We know my version of the virus was trained on horror films. Fear triggers it, however imperfectly. Every time I get sufficiently frightened, or when I gave myself that injection, it activates. That's why I've been passing out."

She gestured with her tablet. "But based on these readings, it's now looking obvious that I was wrong about it at a basic level. I know better now. I think I've figured out what the virus actually does. It's not about healing all ills. I mean, it does that, yes, but only as a side effect. It's actually striving to reset its host to some genetic 'optimal state.' And no, those are not the same.

"Here's the thing, Tycho. That optimal state may be great for Mr. Cooper. It's been peeling away all the damage he's inflicted on himself over the years, restoring him to his ideal being from the template that lives in his cells. But it's a problem for me. My

DNA includes a hardwired disease. The scans I've been running on myself confirm that not only is the virus active in me, it's jump-started the congenital disease that's been quiet for years. The stupid virus has decided that my version of 'optimal' includes my malady being at its peak. Do you follow? I've gone from having months or years before my disease kills me to a little over a week."

The comatose girl had yet to respond to the doctor's questions, and this new revelation hadn't changed that. Jessica nodded to her and continued. "In a perfect world, that wouldn't be a problem. The virus would maintain me at that level, keeping me at my best and not letting the disease progress into a cascade of organ failures. The thing is, it's *not* performing that kind of maintenance. It's clear from the scans that it was working before, both when we left the Box ranch and more recently after I injected myself with adrenaline. Not now. I believe it was terror—of Scatola attempting to kill me and then Mr. Cooper nearly doing the same—that probably jump-started the viral process in me. That's the good news. But, my virus is tied to fear, shaped by thousands of hours of horror films, and that's where, in hindsight, I really screwed up. In order for my version of the virus to stay active, I would have to terrorize myself. Repeatedly. And while the outcome might mean the virus cures my incurable disease and heals me physically, the emotional trauma I'd need to endure would likely drive me crazy and leave me unable to function. All it's really done for me is bring my illness to a peak and run out the clock for me."

The doctor sat and prepped Tycho's arm with an alcohol swab. "But these new readings have given me a wild idea. I should be able to use the virus in your system to fight the version of the virus in my system. Basically, your virus should do its best to reset my genes to what *it* thinks is the optimal version. And yes, I know what you're thinking: your virus will be at odds with the virus already in me and should be enough to keep my disease from progressing, or at least slow it down. I know, Tycho. It isn't perfect and it isn't permanent, but it's all I've got. It may just keep me alive long enough to come up with something better. I guess what I'm trying to say is, thank you."

She withdrew a little over a pint of blood from Tycho's arm. "Sorry to take so much, but the more viral material I have to start with, the faster this will go."

Jessica transferred the blood to the device Doug had cobbled together. She entered the command into her tablet and watched as the propagation system activated and Tycho's blood churned through its reservoirs. On her screen, she watched as the numbers associated with the virus climbed rapidly.

"That should get us started."

The doctor attached a pair of tubes to the system: input and outflow. Next, she prepped both her own arms and inserted the transfusion needles. Finally, Jessica issued a new command and watched as her own blood flowed into one of the remaining reservoirs, where it mixed with the extracted virus. A few moments later, the flow reversed and began to course through the second tube and into her other arm. Jessica winced as the blood seeped back into her own veins. "That got cold fast. I should have told Doug to install a heater."

Knowing all she could do was wait, Jessica sat back in the rickety chair and propped her feet up on the bed. She looked solemnly at Tycho. "If you save me, maybe I can figure out how to save you too. So, for both our sakes, let's hope this works."

CHAPTER SEVENTEEN

Dyrk hailed a pedicab. He climbed into the back and instructed the owner—a beefy three-legged xenon—where to go, then he practically collapsed out of Coop's consciousness.

"Are you all right?" Coop asked.

«I will be. The swap is already so much easier. I'm just catching my breath, so to speak. I'll be fine by the time we get where we're going.»

It was a day for crisscrossing the station. Eventually, the cab stopped in front of a bar. The same bar Dyrk had helped Coop trash a few days before.

"This is not a good idea," warned Coop as he exited the cab and paid the driver.

«Relax, Ben. I've got this.»

"You 'had this' last time we were here. It did not end well. I doubt they're going to welcome me back with open arms."

«Oh, Ben, you underestimate me. Well, you underestimate the powerful tools at my disposal.»

"And what might those be?"

«Ignorant people and free booze.»

"Um..."

Dyrk didn't wait for Ben to finish his thought. With growing ease, he shifted into control of their body and walked down an alley that ran alongside the bar. A dumpster marked the end of the passageway, and an adjacent door opened into the building. He entered a tiny kitchen and passed into the main room, emerging near the stage where a bored-looking woman wandered lazily around the pole at its center. She looked at him with marginal interest before the spark of recognition hit her, and she paused with one shapely leg extended at an impossible angle.

"You again?"

Dyrk gave her what he regarded as a chivalrous nod of his head. «Ma'am. I'm not here looking for trouble.»

"Ha! Oh honey, I think you're one of those people that trouble manages to find whether you look for it or not." She returned to her halfhearted gyrations, and Dyrk strode toward the bar.

As he crossed the floor, conversation ceased in a spreading wave, replaced by angry glances and nervous whispering. The bartender, Lilly, looked up and locked her pretty eyes on him. He could read the curse on her lips from twenty feet away.

Dyrk held his empty hands up in what he believed was a mollifying fashion. It helped his confidence that he had a fresh stun baton strapped to his back like Bruce Willis' gun in that 20th Century classic *Die Hard*. Yeah, like Bruce Willis. Now there was an action hero!

You're going to get us killed, Coop predicted.

Dyrk smiled and whispered his reply for their shared ears alone. «What do we say to the angry mob, Ben?»

Huh?

«'Not today,' Ben. Not today.»

Dyrk turned to the crowd at their tables, raising his voice to be heard over the din.

«Howdy.»

Nobody said anything, but many shifted in their seats to orient on the intruder.

«Tough crowd. Okay. Listen, I know we got off on the wrong foot the other day. But I'm not here to fight. Well, I'm not here to fight any of *you.*»

"Oh shit, not again," the bartender muttered behind him.

«I actually came here to lay low. There are some alien machine assholes called the Box, and they're after me because I'm human, and they think humans are inferior and are meant to be used as slaves and guinea pigs.»

A wave of muttering spread across the room. One man with his nose taped and a pair of black eyes stood up.

"The Box bought up my factory to build their compound. I ain't worked since."

Keep it up, Dyrk.

«Yes, sir. The Box don't care about humans. They don't care about the suffering they cause us. They just come in with their fancy alien tech and their buckets of money and expect to do anything they please. They don't care who they hurt. And it's not just me they're after, no sir. These Box are trying to kidnap a woman who is in hiding. A woman who has done nothing to deserve that kind of treatment. She's come to me for help, and now, if we're going to have any hope of escaping them, we're going to need your assistance. So, please accept my apologies for the other night. I wasn't myself.»

Oh, that's a good one.

«*Thanks, Ben. I was kinda proud of it,*» Dyrk answered internally.

Another man stood up. Coop vaguely remembered his name was Chucky. *Such an unfortunate choice.* His leg was in a cast, and his face reddened as he pointed an accusatory finger at Dyrk. "You broke my leg, asshole. I say we tie you up and hand you over. I bet the Box'll pay good money for you."

«That, sir, would be a mistake,» Dyrk advised.

"Oh, would it?"

«Yes.»

The fat crippled man looked flummoxed, and Dyrk sighed.

«Listen, you of all people know I didn't start the fight the other night. You did. I just finished it. But I really am here to—»

Before Dyrk could finish his appeal, the main door burst open and a small horde of Box spilled into the bar. There had to be at least a dozen extensions. Half of them were the tall, slender models that belonged to Pudełko, but the rest were the shorter, squat versions favored by Caja.

Dyrk glared at Caja's extensions. «I hate that guy.»

Me too. Coop agreed. *Kick his ass.*

«I promise. Believe me, I'm going to enjoy this, Ben.»

Coop was growing more confident in Dyrk's abilities. If he could have put his feet up in his own mind and munched on a bag of popcorn, he would have. He wanted to enjoy watching Caja get his metallic butt handed to him.

The humans looked at the Box horde. They looked at Dyrk.

They seem undecided, Coop noted.

One of the Caja extensions waddled to the front of the pack and pointed a lethal-looking extension toward Dyrk. "We have come to retrieve our human."

Dyrk smirked at the humans and gestured with his arms in an I-told-you-so fashion.

The bar's patrons no longer looked undecided.

You have your audience in the palm of your hand, Dyrk. Coop assured him. *Time to bring them home.*

Dyrk pasted a big grin on his face as he'd witnessed Ben do on several occasions and hopped his butt onto the bar. The rest of the bar's patrons watched him with rapt attention. He looked around dramatically, and a tad dismissively when his eyes passed the Box.

The viral echo in control of Coop's body raised his arms. «Drinks and lap dances are on the house for anyone that brings me a Box head!»

Classy. Very classy.

The crowd roared. Sweat-stained overweight men jumped to their feet. They surged in the direction of the Box like an odorous tidal wave.

The lead Pudełko's mechanical jaw dropped, and Dyrk turned to face the lovely young bartender.

«Do you remember my drink, honey?»

"Martini. Dirtier than a big city whore."

«That's my girl.»

Do I sound like that? Coop asked.

«All the time. It's awesome!» Dyrk watched as Lilly made his drink.

For some reason it is less awesome when someone else does it.

The roar of horny, inebriated, ordinary Joes grew as they slammed into the mass of Box with smelly, concussive force.

They aren't pretty men, Coop observed.

«No. But they are a bunch of glorious bastards. Aren't they?»

"What was that, honey?" Lilly set the martini down by Dyrk's hand just as one of the bar's regulars smashed a carbon-fiber chair across the back of the leading Pudełko.

Yep. They sure are.

The Box seemed unsure of what to do. From the way they hesitated it was obvious they didn't want to hurt the humans, but they had to find ways to fend off their assault.

Dyrk's fingers closed around the stem of the martini glass.

Coop stopped him. *You're not actually going to drink that, are you?*

«Um...I take it you'd prefer I not?»

Lilly gave him a funny look. "Not what?"

Not yet, Coop confirmed. *But make sure to raise it in a toast to your army. That's what I'd do.*

«I'm on it, Ben.»

Dyrk raised the glass in a salutary fashion as he made eye contact with some of his minions. A cry went up from the humans as they continued to smash and harass the Box.

Don't miss your window, Dyrk, the actor advised. *Timing is everything.*

«Right. Thanks.»

"You're welcome, sugar," Lilly responded with a slightly confused look on her face.

Dyrk set his drink down and hopped off the bar. He theatrically cracked his neck before reaching behind into the backpack and drawing forth his stun baton. He tossed his head and ran his fingers through his hair.

Coop objected, *Too much.*

Dyrk dropped his hand. «Right. Got it.»

Get a move on, Dyrk. But stalk. Don't walk. Don't strut. Picking the proper gait is everything. You're playing to an actual audience, not people in a metroplex.

«Strut. Gait. Okay. Thanks, Ben.»

Dyrk squared his shoulders and picked his first target, one of the Caja extensions. It was pressed against the bar, using its superior strength to ward off two large men trying to get their hands around the alien's metal head.

The viral echo stalked over per Ben's instructions and, without breaking stride, twirled his baton and struck the machine's backside. It went limp almost immediately, and the two humans high-fived each other as Dyrk strode past them into the greater melee.

«Showtime!»

Dyrk was lethal. He was an assassin. He was as cool as Antonio Banderas had been when he'd come out of retirement to play that septuagenarian double agent in *Past Your Pasture,* and he knew it. The quintessential action hero.

He could have been an octopus. His limbs moved in every direction at once, dancing about him with Box-felling precision. He never paused as his right hand thrust down, jabbing the baton into a Caja that had been felled by a guy in oil-stained coveralls with a hammer. Dyrk flipped his weapon in an arc over his head and caught it casually in the opposite hand, reversing the grip before striking behind him and notching his first Pudełko. He never even looked at his target.

The Force is strong with you.

«Yeah, it is.»

Be humble, Padawan.

«My bad.»

Despite the rejoinder, Coop was proud of Dyrk. He had ninja skills, and they showed as he hopped onto a table to survey the fight and pick his next target.

To your left. The Pudełko!

Dyrk looked where Ben told him to and saw the problem. One of the Pudełko extensions was getting the better of a small man with a greasy ponytail. The Box had the human on his knees and its mechanical hand locked like a vice around his neck.

The action hero took in the scene and picked his path. He leapt like Errol Flynn to the back of a chair. His toes barely touched the metal before he sprang to the next chair and then onto another table.

That was awesome!

«I know.»

Coop laughed to himself.

Dyrk's hand swept down and picked up a pitcher of beer. He mumbled an apology to the human in the vice-grip as he flung the beer into the Pudełko's face.

Dropping to the floor, Dyrk struck while the Box sputtered. He spun underneath an outstretched mechanical appendage and drove the baton home. The machine jerked and spasmed before it crumpled atop its human captive. Its death grip loosened instantly.

Dyrk looked down with concern but found the ponytailed man grinning back at him from underneath the Box's body. "Man, that was awesome! Go get 'em."

«It was, wasn't it?» Dyrk grinned.

Be cool, Coop reminded him. *Be. Cool.*

Dyrk's grin disappeared, replaced by a steely demeanor and sense of focus, once again the cool professional he'd seen portrayed in countless films.

Dyrk swiveled his head slowly. He was in no rush. He was a wolf among the sheep. He was death incarnate and he could take his time picking his victims. «*I am an apex predator.*»

A Caja shoved a hefty human crashing into Dyrk, and the two men tumbled into a heap.

Way to go, Predator.

«Shut up.»

Dyrk pushed the man aside and jumped to his feet. He squared off against the new threat, whistling and twirling the baton like a Paddy on the beat.

It looked familiar to Coop. *Where did you see that?*

«Sean Connery. *The Untouchables*. Great movie.»

One of the best. Coop sounded impressed. *I'm just surprised you've watched so many older flicks.*

«Dr. Acorns limited me by genre, not by time.»

I'm glad to hear it.

Dyrk yanked his head back as a chair hurtled past his face.

Pay attention! The actor shouted in his own head. *That's my face that almost got messed up.*

«Sorry.»

A man squealed in pain or fear, and Dyrk whirled to his right. The Box seemed to be getting the upper hand. The humans were losing interest in the fight and needed some motivation.

The viral echo rushed the nearest alien, a Caja. The avatar squared off against Dyrk as he charged in. It raised its appendages and spread them wide, ready to capture Dyrk with one crushing embrace.

Dyrk took two more steps before sliding to his knees in a puddle of beer.

Please be careful with my knees. I've got a pin in the left one and I'm gonna feel that later.

But Dyrk didn't pay Ben any attention. His momentum carried him underneath the outstretched metallic arms and in close enough to shove his electric weapon against the Box, causing it to shut down and collapse backward on its robotic haunches even as Dyrk's legs launched him into a somersault over the prone avatar.

He landed in a roll and came up behind another Box, a Pudełko. Its arms were locked in a struggle with three humans, one of whom kept muttering something about free lap dances. Dyrk didn't care. He had plenty of money thanks to the sale to Patel. He *did* care about dispatching the rest of the bastards before he lost his distracting army of inebriated warriors.

He dashed in and shocked the Box while the men wrestled and held it. The extension collapsed under the weight of its attackers, who whooped in delight as they rode it to the floor.

Straight ahead! Coop warned.

Dyrk glanced up. A Pudełko was making short work of one of the few humans the action hero knew well. It was his buddy with the cast.

«How can a guy that big keep getting his butt kicked so easily?»

Dyrk charged. The Pudełko was more desperate than the others. Its pinchers had already drawn blood from the sides of Chucky's neck, and the man's bulging eyes and purple lips said he was in danger of passing out from a lack of oxygen.

As Dyrk closed, the Pudełko lashed out with one of its spare appendages. This one was fitted with a screwdriver-like device and narrowly missed gouging Dyrk's face.

«Whoa!»

Whoa is right! Watch out.

But the Pudełko was clever. It followed up the initial attack with a grasping claw that latched onto the baton. Dyrk resisted, but it was futile. The Pudełko's mechanical strength was too much, and it ripped the weapon from Dyrk's hands.

«Shit!» Dyrk thought.

Ben agreed. *Uh-oh.*

The avatar locked its eyes on Dyrk's face as it shoved the baton into Chucky's sternum. The man's body shook from the electricity. Pudełko pulled it away and then stabbed again, sending the human into convulsions. When he pulled the baton back this time, the man whimpered.

That's not okay.

Dyrk stared daggers at Pudełko. "You're pathetic. You like to think of yourself as a superior life-form. But you're nothing more than an AI bully."

Pudełko let go of its victim and rotated its torso to face Dyrk. Then, like a mechanical bull built by aliens who had never seen an actual bull, it charged forward. Dyrk barely scampered out of the way, dodging between two tables only to catch a glancing blow on the arm from the stun baton.

«Dammit that stings!»

Dyrk shook his left arm and found it still functioned. Mostly. His hand didn't seem too interested in opening or closing. The viral echo shrugged. *«It'll just make for a better story.»*

'Better stories' involve my body remaining intact. There are a lot of ladies that love those fingers. Remember, you're a guest in here!

Dyrk nodded his acceptance of Ben's point and then shrugged free of his backpack as the Pudełko began circling one of the tables to get at him.

The action hero's right hand worked quickly, opening the zipper on the pack. He thrust his hand inside and felt around for the remaining batons. His fingers found one and he opened his hand to grasp it—and Pudełko's pinchers snaked in and snatched the backpack, flinging it away.

«Crap!»

Internally, Coop shook his head.

Dyrk jerked away and just missed being clubbed by the stolen baton. He immediately backpedaled, trying to put distance between himself and the Box. It didn't help. Pudełko used his extra limbs to throw the table aside and closed in on him.

The alien machine swung the baton down at Dyrk's head as it simultaneously slashed across his abdomen with another tool. Dyrk managed an act of contortion worthy of a stage show and narrowly avoided being crushed or cut, although the screwdriver caught his shirt and scored the material in a broad line across his belly.

Dyrk patted his stomach. «See? I told you, pico-fiber for the win!»

Too close! You are so lucky that I eat right and exercise. If I were only above-average looking, I would have had a gut, and even if the fabric didn't cut, the impact would have gouged me wide open. Go get those damn batons back.

«Right.» Dyrk leapt away and ran around another table. He had to dodge again as several humans drove a Caja back with metal bar stools, like a team of old-fashioned lion tamers.

Dyrk put a hand down on the table next to him and launched himself over it. His feet hit the floor on the far side and slid out from him in a puddle of beer. «*Ew. Sticky.*»

He felt, as much as heard Pudełko shove aside the nearby table. Dyrk scrambled away, searching for the discarded backpack. It lay under a table a few meters away, and he lunged for it.

Dyrk's hand grasped the shoulder strap and pulled the bag into his chest. His left hand was still numb, so he flipped the bag over and yanked at the zipper. It opened, and he plunged his good hand inside.

A shadow fell over him.

Dyrk looked up as his fingers found one of the batons. The Pudełko stood above him with a bar stool raised above its head, prepared to slam it down on Dyrk. The avatar radiated malice, and Dyrk had no chance of escaping the blow or striking one of his own in time.

«Oh, shit.»

Oh, shit, is right, Coop agreed.

A voice to the side yelled, "No!" One of the Caja avatars barreled into the Pudełko, tackling it and saving Dyrk. As the two alien machines crashed to the floor, the Caja shouted, "You can't do permanent harm to the humans. We agreed on that."

The two avatars struggled against each other on the floor, and Dyrk stared at them in fascination.

Coop mentally snapped his fingers at the viral echo. *Uh, Dyrk. Please don't waste this opportunity.*

«Good point.» Pulled out of his shock, Dyrk climbed to his feet. He yanked the baton from the pack before slinging the bag across his body.

The Pudełko used its extra limbs to gain an advantageous position. "We didn't agree on an uprising of animals, Caja. We have a destiny to fulfill and I will not see it thwarted by lesser creatures."

«That was rude,» Dyrk grumbled as he strode over and shocked the Pudełko into system failure before it could spew any more of its hateful drivel. The Caja stumbled back, agog, but Dyrk dispatched it before it got to object.

Glancing up from his twofer, he scanned the room, delighted to find that the humans had gained the upper hand on the four remaining avatars. Only one, an enraged Pudełko, seemed to be giving them much trouble.

I don't think you can rely on the Pudełkos exercising any restraint at this point, Coop concluded.

«I think you're right, Ben.» Dyrk ran toward the melee where the avatar had begun swinging its appendages with abandon, cursing at the humans who had it surrounded. A blow connected with one man and he went flying, his face smeared with blood.

«Dammit!» Dyrk shouted as he again leapt onto an empty

chair and used it as a springboard. With effortless grace, he somersaulted up and over the Pudełko. Dyrk landed with a smile and well-earned bravado, pausing to give the Pudełko time to appreciate how artfully it had been outflanked.

Instead, he found himself suddenly ducking a swing from the machine. A section of its torso had spun independently, allowing it to attack Dyrk to its rear without repositioning its whole body to face him.

Dyrk glided backward, avoiding the strike more by luck than skill. «Whoa! That was new.»

The avatar used the momentary surprise to bring the rest of itself in line with the new threat and began swinging its appendages in a vicious pattern. It was mesmerizing, but Dyrk wasn't of a mind to stop and appreciate it. A buzzing saw blade has that effect, even on people born of alien viruses.

Dyrk backed up another step, got his bearings, and adopted a sufficiently unconcerned pose. «You don't scare me, Pudełko.»

"Why not?" the extension asked as it advanced with its menacing menagerie of tools extended in Dyrk's direction.

«Because you fight alone. You've had too many centuries of working by yourself. Pursuing status among your own kind was your only real goal. You've never learned to care for anyone else. Your entire species seems incapable of true teamwork or cohesion.»

"Those are weaknesses."

«Not in a bar fight, they aren't.»

Dyrk stepped sideways as two massive humans rammed one of the bar's carbon-fiber tables into Pudełko's backside and drove the robot six feet away to smash it against the wall. Dyrk winced at the sound of crushing metal before he stepped over to the men who stood over the crumpled machine, panting and grinning.

«Nice work, boys. I'm not sure this is necessary, but…» Just in case, Dyrk leaned over and pressed the stun baton against the flaw in the machine's design, then turned back to the bar in search of another fight. It didn't take him long to find one.

A squat Caja extension stood in the middle of a circle of humans. It held its hands up placatingly, and even appeared to be making attempts to negotiate. It clearly didn't understand humans. Especially drunk humans operating with a vengeful mob mentality.

Dyrk almost felt bad for the Box as the scene unfolded. True to its word, the Caja was determined not to hurt any humans, and this attitude cost it. Dearly. Dyrk didn't even have to engage as the humans pummeled the machine with bar stools, chairs, and even pieces of a nearby Pudełko they had apparently torn apart.

Did Jess ever show you Lord of the Flies? Coop asked.

«No. Was it a good movie?»

It was a classic. But you don't need to watch it now.

«Why?»

Because you're seeing the real thing.

«Ben, I'm not sure I understand.»

I know, Dyrk. Let's try to keep it that way.

The viral echo shrugged Ben's shoulders and watched the brawl become a massacre as the ascendant humans crushed the remaining Box opposition. The litany of metal smashing against metal rang in his ears until, almost as if by agreement, it ended all at once. A small army of sweating, panting humans turned as one to face him. Their faces radiated a mixed sense of satiation and desire that was palpable.

Dyrk took a step back. «Ben, what do they want?»

Blood.

«I can't give them that.»

Then give them booze. It works. Most of the time.

Dyrk nodded and walked casually to the bar, accepting back slaps and grunts of approval from his new friends.

Lilly watched him approach from her place behind the bar.

She did not look pleased. In fact, she looked pissed.

She's angry.

«I didn't need your help figuring that one out.»

I guess that one was obvious. Here, let me handle this.

«*With pleasure,*» agreed Dyrk, already withdrawing to the back of Ben's mind and leaving the actor in control.

Coop did his best to look unconcerned as he leaned over and rested his arms on the bar.

"Sorry about all this."

Lilly crossed her arms across her chest and raised one eyebrow.

«*Uh oh. You sure you got this?*»

"Name your price," Coop persisted confidently.

Lilly looked around at the destruction and laughed without any trace of amusement.

"You can't afford it."

"Try me. I've had a good day. Some investments have paid off."

She quoted him a price and the humans within earshot laughed and gasped. Dyrk didn't know a lot about money, but even he grasped that it was a ridiculous sum. Fortunately, it was a number they could afford.

"Done," promised Coop. "Ring me up. And bring me a... Coke." Her glare was palpable, but he'd earned it. "May I have a Coke? Please."

"You better be able to pay."

"Scout's honor, I've got this. And get those drinks for my friends," he added with a wave of his hand to the crowd. "They've earned it."

A cheer went up from the assembled men. Moments later, as if by magic, the lights and music came back on. The patrons smiled and started to set the furniture up into some semblance of normalcy. Coop let out a deep breath.

"Well, Dyrk. You survived. That wasn't guaranteed. And you've taken down a lot of the Box. But they're not stupid, and there's no way they sent all of their extensions. So, what do you plan to do next?"

«Take the other comm unit from the backpack and let Patel know where he can find another dozen extensions.»

Coop found the comm and called the pawnbroker. "Hey, Patel. Did you find the merchandise I left you at Tartarus? Good. Good. Time for round two. Track this signal and you'll find another dozen waiting for you. Oh, and there's a drink with your name on it too. Just ask for it at the bar. The bartender's name is Lilly."

Lilly had arrived in time to catch the end of the conversation and raised an eyebrow as she set Coop's soft drink in front of him.

He handed her the comm unit. "I've got someone coming to clean up a bit of the mess and haul away your unwelcome visitors. Decent enough guy. His name's Patel. Serve him whatever he wants and put it on my tab, okay?"

"Yeah? How about you settle up for what you already owe." She slid a pad bearing the incredibly inflated bill. Coop signed it with his thumbprint and entered his code to authorize payment. He sipped his cola and watched to ensure the payment went through. When it did, he spun the pad back around to Lilly. "We good?"

The bartender nodded and smiled, which Coop took to mean she'd padded the bill like he'd expected and given herself a well-deserved bonus. "Yeah, all good."

"Great. Well, I'll let you get my friends here the drinks I promised them. Thanks."

Another cheer went up, and a cacophony of voices began ordering drinks. Lilly shouted them down and went to fill their requests.

"Okay, Dyrk. By my count that's got to have been stage four or maybe five of your plan. What now?"

«Now? That's easy, Ben. Now we go get Potato.»

CHAPTER EIGHTEEN

Al studied the data he'd "acquired" from the satellites orbiting above the spaceport. The signatures of Box extensions were easy to track. They looked like nothing else on Titan. What he didn't understand was why iterations of all three versions had departed their ranch, and why in such numbers. In his experience, each type preferred to work alone—if a sapient being capable of spreading its consciousness across multiple robotic bodies could truly be said to be alone. Coordination, much less cooperation, was not their strong suit.

"Unless they find common cause," he murmured. "Something they want more than their independence from one another. Something that drives them beyond reason or choice."

A memory came unbidden: his wife and children, a dozen of his neighbors joining the family in the courtyard, a celebratory feast in honor of his eldest daughter completing another masterwork as a sculptor. What a joy she had been, sweet and kind and generous of spirit, gifted with talent and skill. For her last work, she had carved beauty from the rarest of stones, a substance that only existed in any abundance on the Clusteran home world. That availability, from the Box point of view, had been reason enough to wipe out ninety percent of the population and claim the resource for their own needs.

"Beyond reason or choice," he repeated. "I don't need to know why you're interested in these humans. It's enough to know that you are."

CHAPTER NINETEEN

Coop and Dyrk left the bar and its rowdy but happy patrons behind. Dyrk had put the odds at about eighty-twenty that Patel wouldn't pay for this second allotment of Box extensions, opting instead to collect the avatars and simply stiff Dyrk.

"What are you basing that on?"

«Experience. It's a gut feeling. Trust me, I know how guys like this work.»

"Um... No, you don't, not really. Everything you know comes from the films Jess showed to Potato."

«Your point?»

"The real world is a lot more complicated. Things happen in movies—at least good movies—because they serve the movie. They advance the plot or reveal something about the characters. So your gut feeling is based on the fact that four out of five times having the pawnbroker/fence renege on a deal helped push the story along."

Dyrk pondered that but quickly realized that kind of thinking would call into question *everything* he believed. Better to concede the specific point and move on.

«Huh. Okay. Maybe. I guess I could have the odds wrong. But it

doesn't matter. Money is only a secondary goal. The true purpose of this mission was eliminating as many of the Box as possible, and we nailed that!»

"No argument there. You were amazing."

Mollified, Dyrk guided Ben through a maze of tunnels beneath the spaceport's main concourse until they reached a series of ramps that led back up. They emerged in the commercial arrivals zone, just a few paces from an information alcove and an automated terminal handling rental vehicles.

"Now what?"

«Let me through and I'll show you.»

Coop gave way and Dyrk rushed in. Their shared fingers flew over the terminal's touch screen as Dyrk arranged for a small surface vehicle.

«Huh. Would you look at that? Patel didn't screw us. There's more than six million credits in the account now.»

I haven't seen that many digits in the plus column in a long time. How much is that in U.S. currency back home?

«More than enough to get us back to Earth, with enough left to buy your Malibu beach house several times over.»

Then let's go get Potato and get the hell out of here!

«That's the plan, my man. C'mon.»

Dyrk studied the receipt the terminal had disgorged and followed its printed directions to the designated airlock, where he keyed in the code. The gate whooshed open to reveal a much smaller vehicle than the industrial versions owned by Scatola.

Sexy, Coop jibed.

«It'll get us where we need to go. And it is a lot less conspicuous than the vehicles the Box use. We want to fly under the radar, remember.»

Why does flying under the radar always mean being uncomfortable? And unfashionable?

«Ben. Don't be ridiculous. You're already styling.»

Well, okay, that's fair. But someday I hope to show you what traveling in comfort is all about.

Dyrk got in the driver's seat and sealed the vehicle. The spaceport-side airlock had already closed, and the air was sucked from the vehicle bay. When a green light lit up on the exterior gate, Dyrk keyed in the sequence that opened their exit and admitted what passed for atmosphere on Titan to pour in. He raced the little vehicle out into the orange haze.

«Oh, that's good,» Dyrk remarked.

What is?

«Visibility is especially low today because of the pollution.»

You like smog and pollution?

«I do when I'm engaged in a covert operation.»

You're going to love Los Angeles.

Dyrk chuckled and tapped the communications app on the vehicle's control panel. A moment later, Jessica's face appeared in a small window.

"Mr. Cooper! How are things going? Are you okay? The madam… The manager here said the police were going crazy around town and that she had an inkling you were involved."

«Actually, it's me, Dyrk.»

Dr. Acorns paused and shook her head. "That's going to take some getting used to."

Tell her we're fine.

«I'm going to, sheesh.»

"Going to what?" Jessica asked, perplexed.

«Sorry, Jess. I was talking to Ben.»

"Um, right. I'm still getting used to that too."

«At any rate, we're fine. It was an eventful morning, but so far things are going according to plan. But to keep it that way, I need you to do a couple things.»

"Sure…Dyrk. What do you need?"

«We've secured the funds we need to—»

Jessica interrupted, "I saw. And don't tell me how you got that much money. I'm sure I don't want to know."

Tell her it was a gift from the Box.

Dyrk grinned. «It's all on the up and up,» he promised. «We just pawned some gear the Box will never miss.»

"How did you get your hands on—no, never mind. I don't want to know that either. Go on, what were you saying?"

«I need you to find the most secure and expensive hotel in the spaceport. Make a reservation and tell them to send a limo to transport you and Tycho.»

"Okay, I can do that."

«Good. Now, one more thing. And the timing here is important.»

Jessica stared back expectantly as Dyrk continued.

«I need you to call Scatola.»

"Say what?"

«Trust me here. Wait for the limo to arrive. Then load Tycho. But before you get in the limo and it takes over your comms, call Scatola from your tablet and tell him that you and Ben are about to board a ship and get off this rock. Tell him that if he leaves you alone, you will keep his secrets safe. Then just hang up. Don't let him ask any questions and don't engage him in conversation. Got it?»

Jessica did not look thrilled, but she nodded. "Yeah, I can do that."

Dyrk tapped the comms screen and closed the link to Jessica.

Why are you having her call Scatola?

«We need a diversion to draw the remaining Box away from the ranch. That will give us the chance we need to snatch Potato. Once we have him, we'll be good to go and the Box won't be able to stop us.»

I hope it works.

«Me too, Ben. Me too. Now, I should probably go back to conserving my energy. You drive us toward the ranch and then go past it. Find a place to park where we can see the front gate, and try to conceal us as much as possible.»

Dyrk faded into the background, and Coop suddenly found himself in control of his body, his hands locked on the steering column.

CHAPTER TWENTY

Coop drove. The vehicle turned out to be surprisingly fast for a tiny electric thing. He paralleled the methane river Scatola had pointed out during his first trip. Soon he could see the wall of the Box ranch in the distance. Dyrk's instruction about finding a place to park hadn't made sense—it wasn't like there was much out here. Even so, he scanned the horizon dutifully as he passed the ranch, looking for…something.

The Box weren't the only xenons to lease land and build on Titan's inhospitable surface, but they had secured the closest parcel of real estate. They had also acquired plenty of land on all sides of their compound to ensure they wouldn't have to deal with neighbors, human or otherwise. The only exception had been a small automated fuel depot barely a kilometer from their main gate. That was probably what Dyrk had in mind. Dozens of similar facilities dotted the Titanian surface, and their locations had surely been part of the set of maps the viral echo had absorbed. Half a kilometer out, an automated system pinged Coop's rental vehicle, part of the safety protocol to remind drivers to top off their fuel or charge their power cells before continuing. Coop pulled into the deserted station and swung his vehicle around a full one hundred and eighty degrees to park within range of the automated power coupling. The position also gave him a clear view of the ranch's gate in the distance. He increased the magnification on the forward windshield, centered the camera on the gate, then doubled the magnification again.

"Will this work?" he asked Dyrk.

«Yep. This'll be perfect. Good job, Ben.»

"Now what?"

«Now we wait.»

They didn't wait long. The comm screen beeped to indicate an incoming text message from Jessica's tablet. Coop tapped the key to accept it.

The car is here. Tycho is getting loaded up. I'm about to make the call. Good luck. – Jessica

«Alrighty, Ben. Get ready.»

"I was born ready."

«Good line. Classic.»

"I'm a classic kind of guy."

«At least you didn't say classy.»

"Dyrk?"

«Yeah, Ben?»

"Shut up."

«Okay.»

Moments later, the gate in the security wall opened. The unmistakably arrogant silhouette of a Scatola avatar crossed the open space from the ranch's nearest habitat module. Its legs churned dust as it sped away from the compound toward the spaceport.

"Damn. He's fast."

«Avatars don't get tired. They're made for hard work even when they get dressed up pretty-like.»

"Noted."

Another avatar emerged from the ranch. Then another. In the end, a group of three avatars—stiff Scatola, lanky Pudełko, and round Caja—ran out the gate and tore up the road. None of them paid any attention to the car parked at the refueling station a kilometer away.

"They didn't take a vehicle. How do they plan to bring me, Tycho, and Jessica back without one?"

«They don't. They never had much use for you, pal, and less for poor Tycho. And apparently Dr. Acorns' utility has also come to an end.»

A minute ticked by. Another.

"I think the coast is clear," Coop suggested.

«Yeah. Let's roll.»

Coop transferred payment for the power-up and disconnected from the pump. He put the little vehicle in gear and headed to the compound.

«Go ahead and pull up to the gate.»

"If you say so." Coop did as instructed, and a moment later the gate's control screen flashed with an automated query for identification from the Box security system. The armature with the retinal scanner extended toward his window.

"This is your plan?" Coop's voice in their shared head sounded incredulous. "To submit to a retinal scan? Did you forget that Scatola programmed a bio-block into the security system? Literally anyone else on Titan can get through more easily than I can."

«Have some faith in me, man. I've healed our bones, replaced our liver, and wiped out the degradation of our telomeres to reverse our aging. You think my mojo can't handle tweaking our retinas? I just need a little extra juice, is all.»

"Don't think I don't notice you keep using the word 'our.' And what do you mean 'extra juice'?"

«Yeah... Because if I screw this up, the Box will probably come back and begin cutting into us to find out the secret behind the virus.»

Cooper's heart rate jumped at the suggestion of vivisection, and Dyrk flashed him a mental grin.

«Thank you. That's just the juice I needed.»

Before he could repeat his request for an explanation, Coop cried out in pain. It was like a pair of red-hot pokers had been driven into his skull. He brought his hands to his eyes but as quickly as it began, the burning sensation in his sockets had already ended.

«That's it. We're good to go now. You can check in with the scanner now.»

"What did you do?"

«I changed our identity. At least, as far as retinal identification is concerned.»

"How?"

«I altered our retinas.»

"Altered them to what?"

«Right now, we're a match for Thomas Doyle.»

"Never heard of him. Who the hell is he?"

«He's a delivery guy for Titan Express. I picked him up when I was scanning records at the data center. He's been dropping by the ranch at least once a week, bringing in supplies Dr. Acorns needed. He's pre-approved in the Box system.»

Coop peered through the window as prompted and stared into the retinal scanner. Whatever Dyrk had done must have worked because the gate opened. Coop drove through to the garage at the first of the habitats. He parked and waited as the Box system responded to the vehicle's protocol handshake and swapped the local atmosphere for a more suitable blend, then exited the rental car and stepped through the airlock into the habitat. Inside the interior corridor, he stopped and listened.

"The place seems empty."

«That was the plan. Get a move on. We need to get Potato and get out of here before the Box realize they've been tricked and come back.»

Coop hustled down the hallway. He looked left. He looked

right. He jumped at a couple of shadows that proved to be only shadows. He wove through the corridors until he arrived at the grotesquerie that served as Potato's posh and oversized abode. After all the action, he was almost disappointed to make it without incident. Almost.

Coop found Potato at the far end of the room. The adorable little guy was perched atop his favorite ottoman, doing what Potato did best: nothing.

Ben started across the room.

«Coop. Something isn't right.»

Cooper stopped mid-stride. "What do you mean?"

«It's Potato. He isn't...breathing. Move over!»

Dyrk shoved Coop's consciousness aside and took control of their shared body. He rushed to Potato's side and knelt to inspect the alien creature. Up close, the problem became clear. It wasn't Potato. It was a furry mockup. A fake Potato.

«Dammit. We're fucked.»

The door back to the corridor slammed shut and Dyrk jumped to his feet. Spinning around, he found the three musketeers of alien-assholedom glaring at him. Each held what could only be described as ray guns in their robotic hands. That was just plain crazy. It made no sense to have, let alone use, blasters in an airlocked environment. Dyrk was about to point this out when Scatola spoke first.

"Did you truly believe we'd abandon the ranch? All of us? And if you're here, Mr. Cooper, not just still alive but looking healthier than ever, it must surely mean that Dr. Acorns' treatment has proved successful. Given these facts, not only are you *not* boarding a ship home, but I seriously doubt she is either. Caja, call the port and give a passcode to their security detail to share with our extensions when they arrive. They'll come back and then we'll secure the ranch from further mischief. Pudełko, take Mr. Cooper in tow. There's a table in Dr. Acorns' former infirmary that he knows well. Strap him down. I will be along shortly, after I review the last entries from her research logs. Let us see if we cannot take the doctor's work to the next level and begin to decipher the message in the virus we've waited so long to heed."

«There is no message,» shouted Dyrk.

"I would expect you to say that. You're an ignorant member of a stupidly young and barely sentient species. You're probably only concerned for your own well-being and hoping to avoid pain. Alas, there will be no avoidance. We will have the message from you if we have to strip it from your body one cell at a time."

«Like hell, you will.»

Pudełko pulled the trigger on its gun, and Dyrk felt a sting burn his leg. When he looked down, he saw the end of a dart sticking out from his thigh.

«Huh. Tranq gun. Not a ray gun after all…»

CHAPTER TWENTY-ONE

As the drug took hold, Coop found himself back in control of his own body and heard Dyrk gasp inside his head. This was followed by a flurry of sensory bursts and blurs unlike anything Dyrk had shared so far. The mental sound was musical and tasted of maple syrup.

«We're blissing out, buddy. The drug they've hit us with is some alien cocktail that makes the tranq darts from the spaceport cops look like sugar water. I'll try to absorb as much of the effects as I can, but that's going to take all my focus. You're on your own until I can purge it from us. This is your stage now. You're on, Ben.»

Dyrk faded even as Coop realized his brain was doing its best to shut down. Words seemed like a good idea. He vaguely remembered having an appreciation for them, and thought he might one day be able to string them together again. Time was a funny concept too. He was having a hard time keeping track of what was happening in the now. *Focus.* Somewhere, Dyrk was trying to help, and Coop had to be ready, didn't he? Ready to use whatever aid the viral echo threw his way. He became aware that Pudełko had already begun dragging him down the hallway. Coop had a sudden emptiness in his mind he'd never noticed before. He was all alone in his head, same as he'd been for his entire life, minus the past few days since Jess had injected him with her crazy virus. Same as everyone else was. A wave of melancholy washed over him. All alone. Either because of the sudden emotion or the drug, Cooper's limbs turned rubbery. Pudełko soon reached the lab and tossed Coop onto the examination table. When the avatar grasped the table's straps and moved to secure him in place, it was the most natural thing in the world for Coop to let his body go limp. He slid off the table and crumpled to the floor just as Pudełko tried to tie him down.

"Do not resist, Mr. Cooper. You will find I have much less patience for your antics than the others."

Instead of replying, Coop managed to roll under the table, buying himself some time. Despite visions of sugar plums dancing in his head to the smell of a Sousa march, his mental lethargy had cleared enough to begin working through his predicament.

Predicament, that's a funny word, the way it rolls around in the mouth before jumping out in a mad rush. No, wait, more focus. Focus!

Getting off the table had removed the immediate threat, but it wasn't a total solution. He was pleased to have reached that conclusion. Next, he decided the floor was not particularly comfortable. That realization led to another: he had no intention of being vivisected or any other version of hell the Box wanted to concoct for him. He was over their bullshit! With great effort, he rolled onto his side from beneath the table and away from the clumsy avatar, who had just managed to bend down and wedge its long frame in its pursuit.

The drug from the Box tranq continued to mess with Coop's head. He experienced a sudden loss of proprioception, missing the feedback from his limbs. His hands and feet seemed to belong to someone else, much like when Dyrk was in control of his body and Coop was just watching them do things. Except Dyrk was gone. As best he could, Coop used the table to haul himself upright. His left hand found a perch on some menacing piece of medical equipment, one of several diagnost-iframa-thinga-doodles that had fed its data directly to Jess' tablet. But Jess wasn't here and he didn't want any data. Coop stared at his hand like it was a stranger's, then at the hardware, and wondered what else it might be good for. He asked his other hand for a favor, and it reached up and hooked around some flange on the thing. The double grip made it possible to pull himself up further, and he managed not to flop his body back across the examination table.

"Okay, better, but not great. This is not where I want to be."

Coop rolled again and felt something pressing against the small of his back as he leaned on the table. It was hard and round and it hurt.

"Oh...the baton."

His brain continued to struggle against the drug in his system, and he regained the sense that his hands and feet were on the same page with him. Maybe the chemicals were washing out of his system. Or maybe Dyrk was doing it. It was hard to tell and the progress was slow going either way. Eventually, a profound insight blossomed in his awareness. He could use the baton to escape! He fumbled at his back until his fingers found purchase on the handle, extricating the weapon from his waistband. He leaned out over the examination table and saw Pudełko's metal chicken legs sticking out. The avatar was trying to wrestle itself out from under the table, but all the fancy extra limbs along its torso were useless in this position.

"This is too easy."

But even drugged, decades as an actor had made Coop a practical man. He'd done some improv. He knew how to seize opportunities as they presented themselves. Waste not, want not. *Carpe diem* and all that. He reached down and, after a few failed attempts, managed to bring the baton in line with the correct spot on the Box's exterior. Coop struck and Pudełko froze as its consciousness was forced from its mechanical body.

"That'll do, Donkey. That'll do. Phase one complete." Visions of alien dissection had long since replaced the sugar plums in his head. Just as well. They were a much better motivator, and he remembered that he needed to get his butt in gear if he wanted to avoid being strapped on that table again.

Wobbly, but more ambulatory than when he'd come in, Coop made his way across the room and hid behind the door. He fell twice along the way, a sure sign that navigating the hallway and attempting an escape from the compound probably wasn't in the cards, at least not before Dyrk managed to absorb or break down or do whatever he was doing to the drug the Box had shot him with. So really, all Coop could do was wait.

I can do this. It's no different than waiting between scenes on a set. It takes as long as it takes. I can do this.

Time stretched and lost meaning. That realization jump-started his thinking a bit. After more waiting and more muddled cognition, Coop produced a new plan. He marveled at its simplicity, confident that Dyrk would approve. He'd lean there against the wall and ambush Scatola when the jerk came through the door. All he had to do was hold the baton at the ready.

It was a good plan, but disconnected from reality. After only a few seconds of holding himself poised and alert, Coop's knees grew so watery that it was difficult to stand up. Despite that, a blissful euphoria had begun tickling his brain. He knew it was the drug from the dart, but that distinction didn't seem to matter. He felt really, really good. Confident. Powerful. Frankly, he wasn't sure he needed the baton. Maybe all he really needed was a nap. Yeah, a nap sounded good.

Coop continued to debate the merits of lying down and catching some sleep until the door opened. Scatola marched right past him into the room and stopped in front of the examination table.

The Box extended his arms. "Pudełko. Why are you on the floor? Where is Mr. Cooper? What are you playing at?"

Despite the artificial bliss, a smidgeon of pragmatism broke through Coop's muddled state and demanded he take Scatola out before his much-desired nap. He stepped away from the wall and flung himself at the Box's back in one of those it-seemed-like-a-good-idea-at-the-time moves. The result was less than heroic.

He draped himself like a cape over the avatar's shoulders, dropping his stun baton. A pang of sadness rippled through him, but only for a moment. Coop decided he wasn't without other weapons.

The actor smashed his fist into the side of Scatola's head. He did it again and again. He kicked his feet weakly against Scatola's legs and generally made a nuisance of himself, even if he didn't actually manage any damage. The absurdity of his actions bubbled up to his awareness and Coop laughed and laughed, though he didn't stop his attack. He even head-butted the machine one time, but it hurt too much, so he resumed using his hands. Finally, having tired of the pathetic display, Scatola reached back over his shoulders and grabbed the human. The Box flipped him up and over, and Coop landed hard on the examination table.

"Ow," was his only comment as the air whooshed from his lungs.

"I don't know why I allow you to disappoint me so, Mr. Cooper. One cannot reasonably expect a lower-tier life-form such as yourself to understand the greater imperatives of the universe. It was patently ridiculous of me to expect you would adhere to a contract when your baser motivations were at stake." Scatola shook his synthetic fists at the sky, reminding Coop of dozens of mediocre bad guys in films he'd done.

This was usually the point where the villains were so distracted by their self-indulgent monologues that the hero could seize the day. *Dyrk's not the only action hero in this body, dammit.* Coop rolled off the table from the same side he'd climbed up earlier. It wasn't graceful, but it put the table between him and a Box he needed to keep away from.

Coop shook his head and tried again to clear the effects of the drug from his mind. It didn't work, but at least it dissolved the nagging desire for a nap and reminded him he needed to get the hell away from Scatola. He grabbed onto the body scanner he'd used to haul himself up off the floor previously.

It was nice to find such a reliable piece of machinery. Coop patted the machine. It swiveled under his weight, and he threw himself on it in a desperate attempt to stay on his feet. Coop's toes left the floor as the armature swung him around the examination table in a lazy arc right toward Scatola.

The Box adopted an aggrieved posture, with his hands on his hips and his head cocked to the side.

The scanner slowly drifted closer as Coop pumped his feet, kicking the air in an attempt to find purchase.

Scatola waited. He had an amused and almost patient look on his smug face as Coop inched closer. The armature buckled under Coop, just a little. Despite its bulk, it was a delicate piece of machinery, intended to pivot and swivel as needed to achieve the best position to run its scans and *not* to be weight-bearing. It lurched and dropped him an inch. The movement hurt his chest, but it didn't stop him from getting closer to the Box.

"No good."

Coop wiggled his feet and found the floor. A fresh rush of euphoria hit his brain. It was misplaced—his writhing only accelerated his trajectory toward doom.

"Abort! Abort! This is not the way you were meant to go, Coop." He pressed both feet against the floor and shoved off.

Scatola reached out and placed one hand on the back of Coop's shirt.

"A good try, Mr. Cooper. Futile. But I suppose your desire to survive is a powerful one."

The scanner buckled again, jostling man and avatar and

surprising them both. An instant later, it ripped out of the ceiling. Coop fell against the mechanical arm and cracked a rib as his torso collided with the metal. Scatola leaned over to keep his grip on the actor and might have succeeded if the scanner's entire frame hadn't come tumbling down on top of him.

Several hundred pounds of proprietary medical technology crushed Scatola and slammed him down on top of Coop, who cried out in pain.

A moment passed without the Box speaking or moving. Weird. Coop took stock of the situation. He was on the floor, pinned down by Scatola and a mountain of metal. He was alive though, and as near as he could tell, Scatola wasn't.

"Well, that's a start."

Coop wiggled his feet, delighted to find them fully functional. He did the same with his arms. He felt sluggish, but all his parts seemed to be working. Slowly and painfully, he wedged, pushed, and dragged himself out from under the pile. Even without the drug in him, he doubted he'd have managed to go much faster.

Once free of the crushing weight, Coop lay on his back and gingerly poked at his aching ribs. They hurt. Badly. Each breath made him want to vomit and scream and maybe even pass out. But breathing was way better than the alternative.

He carefully rolled onto his side and then his knees. He placed a hand against his rib cage and managed to stand.

"One small step."

Once he was on his feet again, he looked back to see where he'd been. Scatola looked well and truly crushed. The base had been bolted to the ceiling to hold the full weight of the scanner, and it had fallen directly atop the Box's torso. The sharp corner of the plate had penetrated Scatola's protective shell, piercing the hardware beneath.

Coop did not feel any remorse. He began to giggle. It hurt a lot.

"Hey, Dyrk! Dyrk, you there? Two down. Not bad for an understudy, right?"

No response. That made Coop feel a little sad, but he had a mission to complete. He had to rescue Potato, and he'd do it. "For Dyrk."

The actor was armed with newfound determination that, had he been clearheaded enough to assess it, demonstrated his thinking was actually still quite muddled. He shuffled to the area beneath the exam table and found the stun baton behind the rubble. He picked it up on his third try and made for the door. On the way there, he caught a glimpse of his reflection in the window.

He looked hurt but rugged. Sure, he was injured, but he wasn't defeated. He looked good. Like a hero.

"Ben-mother-fucking-Cooper to the rescue, ladies and gentlemen."

Coop winked at his reflection and went in search of Potato. It was time to fulfill the role he'd been born to play.

CHAPTER TWENTY-TWO

Coop hobbled from room to room, growing more determined to find and rescue Potato with every agonizing step. Potato deserved better. Dyrk did too. However inadvertently, the fucking Box had made the viral echo. They'd created him and unleashed him, and then they'd tried to hunt him down like a dog. They pretended they revered the virus, just as they seemed to revere Potato. It was all bullshit, though. The Box just used them as a means to their arrogant, misguided ends.

"Assholes," Coop muttered. He opened the door to the communications room and found Caja.

"Damn, I forgot about number three. Stupid drug."

The remaining Box was half Coop's height but three times his girth, and it carried Potato in its metal hands. Potato was just chilling with his absurd tongue lolling out his furry face. Although he was still addled by the drug, Coop managed to draw the stun baton from his waist. He even held it from the right end, after a moment.

"Okay, Caj... Cajones, it's just me and you. Hand over the furball or face my righteous wrath!"

Caja glared at him. "I told Scatola your kind would only be trouble, that we would be better to just ignore your species entirely. But no, he thought you brought something new to the equation. Even modeled his avatars on your form. Pointless, and worse still, a waste of our time. And you, Mr. Cooper, you are the worst of your kind. All you've done since we brought you here is run away. I will put an end to that now. We don't need you completely intact to study the effects of the virus. Humans are so fragile. A tendon here, a kneecap there, and you'll not run away ever again."

Caja shoved Potato under one mechanical arm and advanced.

But Potato wanted no part of it. The little fuzzball began to squirm. It actually writhed and wiggled. For any other life-form it would have been a pathetic mockery of action, but for Potato, any motion was revolutionary. It actually seemed excited. Motivated even. Coop never would have used that word to describe Potato. The little alien had always acted like a professional lump. It had more in common with a doorstop than any other living creature. Sloths looked ambitious by comparison.

"Well, I'll be damned." Coop watched as Potato continued to resist with greater intensity.

Caja stopped and stared at the twisting lump of hair under its arm. It gently poked at Potato with one of its mechanical extensions, as if trying to understand what was happening. It made sense—Coop was shocked at the display, and he'd only known Potato for less than a week. Caja had spent centuries with the creature, and in all that time Potato had never worked off more calories than required for minimal breathing.

It was incredible. It was also the perfect distraction, though it took Coop's drug-addled mind a few extra seconds to pick up on that.

He attempted to drop and roll, intending to come up behind Caja. The pain from his rib turned it into an uncoordinated collapse to the floor. He grabbed one of Caja's legs with both hands and pulled himself forward. It wasn't ideal, but at least he had the Box's own bulk for cover.

Caja's torso began to turn, bringing Coop back into its view, but Potato forced it to stop. The creature's gazillion little legs scrambled wildly against the avatar's metal surface. Potato seemed to be trying to climb up and over Caja to regain sight of Coop.

"Aww. That is adorable. I love that little guy."

Caja flailed around, trying to maintain its grip on the secret to its race's existence, but Potato wouldn't cooperate, not one little bit.

Coop seized his chance and struck at the Caja's left butt cheek with the baton.

Nothing happened.

Coop shook his head, trying to focus.

He struck again. No luck.

Caja continued to fumble with Potato even as it became aware of the threat Coop's baton posed. The Box shuffled its feet and turned. Coop switched his grip to its other leg, jerking around like a little kid trying to hang onto a seat on a merry-go-round as he waved the baton.

He struck at Caja's rump, missing over and over again. The broader base of this avatar model made it harder to find the right spot. He hadn't had this much trouble at the bar, but back then the Box's cocktail hadn't been messing with his eye-hand coordination. His arm was growing tired, and every step Caja took sent a bolt of pain lancing out from Coop's broken rib.

"Go down, damn you!"

Coop struck again. And again. He flailed the baton against Caja's backside as the pain in his own side increased.

ZZZZTTTT!

The baton finally hit home, and Caja came to a halt.

Coop fell off the Box's leg and collapsed. "Oh, thank God," he panted.

Above him, Potato's cute little eyes stared down at him from his perch on the avatar's shoulder.

"Hi there, little buddy."

Potato's tongue plopped out in response, dangling a ridiculous distance.

"Yep, the ladies are gonna love you."

Coop eased himself to a sitting position and then used Caja's frame to pull himself fully upright, wincing from his injured rib.

Potato jumped off Caja's shoulder and landed against Cooper's chest. The actor grabbed him and fell down again, crying out when he struck the floor. He needed a full minute of labored breathing before he could get past the pain.

"You're lucky you're cute. You know that right?" He spoke through clenched teeth as he stared into Potato's eyes.

The pain receded. In seconds it vanished entirely. Maybe it was the drugs, or maybe it was his victory over the three Box, but Coop felt really good. When Potato began to lick his face, he knew all was right in the world.

Pressure built in the base of his skull, and a presence expanded in a spot he'd never noticed in his mind before.

Potato seemed excited and began dancing on Coop's chest.

«Ben? Can you hear me?»

"Dyrk! Welcome back. Are you okay? You sound weird."

«Thanks. I'm still working at purging bits and pieces of the drug, but I'll be fine. And hey, Potato really likes you.»

"Well, yeah. At least more than the Box, for sure. But Jess never said anything about getting an alien tongue bath. Remind me to read my contract more closely next time. What's gotten into the little guy? He's usually a total lump. Why's he so…animated?"

«Beats me. If I had to guess, he's sensing there's another entity with

its virus. I told you we were kin. The poor thing has been alone for how many centuries? It's never had any reason to want to move before now. Come on, let's get out of here. The good doctor will have settled into our new lodging by now. We've got Potato, and we should go join her.»

CHAPTER TWENTY-THREE

Dyrk's return had brought a quick end to the pain in Coop's side. The actor stretched gratefully as he walked down the hall with Potato cradled affectionately in his arms.

"That feels good," Coop remarked. "I'm glad you're back."

«Me too. Happy to be of service.»

"I have to hand it to you. Your plan worked. Well, mostly. We rescued Potato. But, now what?"

«Now we need to get off this damn rock. The first step is to get into our car and link up with Jessica and Tycho.»

"Won't the Box keep coming after us?"

«Probably, but we have two things we didn't have yesterday. We have Potato, and we have lots of money. I suspect those will be enough to get us back to Earth unharmed.»

"Well, money makes the world go around. Let's just hope the same rule applies here on Titan."

«If I had control of our hands, I'd high-five us right now.»

"I appreciate the sentiment."

Coop arrived at the door to the garage. The green light above the door was on, indicating that the terrestrial atmosphere was in place and it was safe to enter. Coop opened the door and strode in, whistling a jaunty tune.

"You're supposed to be at the spaceport, Mr. Cooper."

Scatola stood in the middle of the garage.

"Oh, come on!" Coop stamped his foot.

Scatola chuckled in his mechanical British-villain accent. It was really cheesy. "I would like to give you credit, Mr. Cooper. Your effort to distract and divide us via disinformation was well played. Admirable even, for a lower life-form."

"Uh, thanks?"

"You correctly diagnosed the limits inherent in our system of conscious extensions and used it to your advantage. It was clever. Clearly, I seriously underestimated you where cunning is concerned. But even lesser animals of brute intelligence are capable of deception when their lives are on the line. I should have expected no less."

Coop rolled his eyes. "You really know how to flatter a guy."

Scatola paused. "It is not my intent to flatter, Mr. Cooper. I was merely stating a series of unfortunate facts. Our current situation is as much a failure of vision on my part as it is a success on yours. I assume you were the source of the 'tip' I received that has resulted in so many of our extensions going missing? I see now that I allowed my desire to reclaim you and Dr. Acorns to override my better judgment and operational protocols. I failed to grasp the meaning behind the lack of updates from the extensions that went chasing after you at the pair of spaceport venues. When it finally occurred to me to check, I was halfway to the spaceport and found I could only synchronize with one of my other extensions, the one here at the ranch. Imagine my surprise to find him chasing you in the laboratory before you crushed him underneath the body scanner and severed the connection to his central processing unit."

"That must have been quite the shock."

Scatola shook his head.

"When I realized what was happening, I transferred full awareness back to this extension, which was racing with the others toward the spaceport. It was obvious we were being diverted. Ben Cooper could not be boarding a ship to return to Earth if he was back at the ranch. I assume you have somehow destroyed all of our other extensions?"

"Something like that."

Scatola gave a reluctant grunt of admiration. "Again, I underestimated you. But your little fiction has failed. When I realized what you had done, we all turned around and came back to the ranch, and there was your vehicle parked in the garage. I have conferred with my colleagues. We are in complete agreement that this entire phase of our research has been a waste. We are leaving Titan. Today."

"That's great. Sorry I can't say it's been fun, but you and the others have yourselves a safe trip."

Scatola smiled. It was an evil smile, far more sinister than anything Copper had in his actor's repertoire of expressions. Then again, who would want to cast Ben Cooper as a villain? His face was way too handsome for that.

"No, Mr. Cooper. You misunderstand me. Neither Caja nor Pudełko are taking a trip. They've gone back to their respective habitats and by now are uploading all of their research data to send it home. As soon as they're done, they'll implode their habitats so that no Box technology remains to fall into lesser hands."

"I don't get it. Why blow up their stuff if they're not leaving?"

"I said they are not taking a trip, but they are most certainly leaving, Mr. Cooper. They'll arm self-destruct sequences in their extensions and likewise upload their consciousness to the null-space transceiver and—what is your expression? Be home in time for supper?"

"I would have said, 'Get the fuck out of Dodge.' But what about you? Why aren't you 'beaming' back?"

"I should think the primary reason would be obvious even to

a being of your limited intelligence. Someone has to physically transport Potato back to Box space."

"Yeah, that won't be happening. So if you haven't got another reason to stay, feel free to upload your ass out of here."

"But I do, Mr. Cooper. My secondary purpose here is to hurt you. Because of you, I have lost status and respect among my peers. I will forever be known among my kind as the Box who was duped by a human. The humiliation is beyond your comprehension. But perhaps there is a possibility for redemption. The maladies you possessed when I acquired you on Earth have clearly vanished. And Potato is no longer the sluggish creature he has been since we found him millennia ago. Something of Dr. Acorns' treatment has indeed worked."

Coop shrugged. "So?"

"So, I intend to pull your limbs from your torso and place what's left of you into a packing crate. I'll even stuff Potato in with you for company. My research is taking a new turn, Mr. Cooper. If Potato's virus is indeed active in what's left of your body, I'm sure I'll be able to tease out its secrets. And when I do, my failure here on Titan will be written as the misunderstood prelude to my ultimate triumph. Once that happens, I will finally put you out of your misery, quickly and without further pain. All debts paid. Now, do both of us a favor and set Potato down."

A cold sweat ran down Coop's spine. He really did not want to be cut up and experimented on. He wasn't afraid of dying, but Scatola was promising something much worse than death. Nope. There had to be a way out of this.

«Psst! Coop. Hang in there, man. I'm trying to come all the way back.»

Well, do it faster.

«I'm close. Just stall him.»

"Yeah… no. Sorry, Scatola. That plan doesn't work for me. If I let go of Potato, you'll just start in on that whole ripping off my arms and legs thing."

Scatola shrugged. "I'm going to do that anyway. Why delay the inevitable?"

"First off, because like most humans, I always avoid pain for as long as possible. We're incredibly well adapted for procrastination related to unpleasant activities. Second, because maybe I have a different plan."

"A plan? You must think I'm a fool, Mr. Cooper. You are out of options. There's nowhere for you to run. You cannot overpower me. There is no convenient medical apparatus for you to drop on me. What could you possibly do that changes anything?"

"Maybe... this!" Coop took a step back and, as he had in his role of quarterback in *Gridiron Heist,* took advantage of the height of the garage's ceiling and threw Potato in an arc that would carry him over the Box's head.

Scatola lunged to catch the creature and Coop dove between the Box's legs in a now well-practiced move. He spun as he passed through them, arriving on the other side looking up the Box's backside. With his head much clearer now, he gripped the stun baton with both hands and drove it into place. In the next instant, he scrambled to get into position before Potato hit the floor. It was a near thing, but Coop caught the immortal alien in his outstretched hands. Potato found the whole game delightful and rewarded Cooper with another face licking.

«*I could have done that for you,*» Dyrk insisted. His words were still a little slurred. «*If you'd have kept him talking another five minutes, I would have.*»

"Next time," Coop promised.

«*Ooooh, there's going to be a next time? Outstanding!*»

CHAPTER TWENTY-FOUR

The luxury shuttle stopped in front of the *Palais Titan* hotel, and a small army of liveried bellhops and attendants descended upon the vehicle. Jessica could barely get down from the hotel's limo without stepping on the toes of some eager young man. It was like a college party but less creepy. Not that she'd attended many parties during her college years. As a pre-med double major, there'd been no time for nonsense games with frat boys, however attractive they might have been. And yet, for just a moment, the pair of muscled, tough-looking men hovering on the edges of the action gave her pause.

"Good day, miss." A short, wiry man bowed to her. He was clothed like the others, but with the addition of gold fringe epaulets marking him as their leader. "Welcome to the *Palais*. I'm Jared, and I am the lead steward for the presidential suite."

"Hello." Jessica was a little flustered by all the attention. "I need to see to my...patient." The steward responded with a perfunctory nod, as if he regularly picked up unconscious women from whorehouses, and led her around the shuttle as Jessica looked anxiously for Tycho. Jared's regard for her had changed, as if the word "patient" had caused him to recategorize her from young woman to physician. If she wasn't so concerned about Tycho, she'd have spared a moment to roll her eyes.

The team of bellhops gently lifted the comatose Tycho from the hatch at the rear of the limo. They carefully secured her on a hover bed held in place by another bellhop.

Jessica wasn't worried, but she decided to check on Tycho anyway. She ran a quick diagnostic on her tablet and, as expected, everything was fine. She breathed a little easier anyway.

The steward never left her side. "Is everything to your satisfaction?"

"Yes, very much. Thank you. But I was wondering, why does a hotel keep hospital-grade float beds on hand?"

Jared smiled and nodded. "Every so often, we have a guest suffering from null-space syndrome. The neurologic effects are severe but can be managed with time."

Could that explain Dyrk?

"Null-space syndrome. Of course. Thank you, Jared. You just gave me an idea I very much needed."

Jared looked a little confused, but he rolled with it. He was probably used to odd guests saying odd things.

"My pleasure, doctor. Now, if you'll follow me, I'll be happy to show you to your suite. Your patient will be right behind us." He gave a meaningful look at the bellhops pushing the hover bed.

"Okay." Jessica's mind raced as she followed him. She did her best to act like she was used to the attention and treatment, but she found it difficult to stop looking over her shoulder at the squad following her with Tycho in tow. Something occurred to her. "Did you say we're going to the presidential suite?"

"Yes, ma'am. The gentleman who upgraded your room demanded it. I am told he was quite adamant about your security requirements, and insisted that we treat you as we would any other dignitary. And might I add, it is always my pleasure to do so."

"Umm...right. Sure."

Jared led the way across the crowded lobby. Jessica felt dozens of eyes following her across the marbled floor. Surely this kind of attention was the complete opposite of what Dyrk would have wanted. She noticed the two dangerous-looking men had quietly, but none too subtly, formed a cordon between her group and the rest of the hotel's patrons. It made her feel better.

As they approached a pair of bronze elevator doors, Jared subtly tapped on a wrist controller and the doors opened to welcome them inside without pause. When the doors closed, only Jessica, Tycho, Jared, the two bellhops pushing the hover bed, and the two security men were inside. It was a snug fit. When the doors opened on their floor, two more security personnel—a human woman and a beefy-looking xenon—stood in the hallway.

Jared led the way and flung open the doors to the suite.

"Wow," Jessica whispered. "This certainly is...presidential."

She oversaw the bellhops as they transferred Tycho to one of the bedrooms, then she ushered them from the suite and closed and locked the door behind them. All the equipment she'd brought from Madam Zana's had been set out in the suite's foyer. It beckoned to her. There was so much left to do.

CHAPTER TWENTY-FIVE

Back in the lobby, Alhiz'khlo'tam, a.k.a. Al, had watched as the young doctor and her patient were escorted to the elevator. Jared, who had taken bribes from Al for years, led the way. A team of security personnel flanked the party, contracted from a firm Al owned via a human-faced shell corporation. When the elevator doors closed and the group was safely on their way to the hotel's best suite, he took a last sip of his drink and smiled.

"If deals like this keep falling in my lap, I may have to reconsider my belief in divinity. And then question why a deity would look out for me."

The alien chuckled in his throat, imagining his wife's winsome grin at the idea of him pondering theology at all. The chuckle died away. Her smile, like so much else, was lost forever. He stood and straightened his suit. Satisfied that all was well in hand, he strode from the hotel to check on the rest of the arrangements he'd set in motion, both those Cooper had requested, and some the human knew nothing about.

Opportunities were presenting themselves as they had never before. Al understood he might have to call in a few favors, might even have to extend one or two of his own, but if there was even a chance of affecting the Box, perhaps even foiling some of their plans, he had to take full advantage of the possibility.

CHAPTER TWENTY-SIX

Coop walked Potato over to the car and placed the little furball in the passenger seat. He patted it on the head, ran his fingers through the alien's blue and green fur, and shut the door. As he walked around the car to get in and drive away, he stopped and took in the stationary avatar. The last extension of Scatola.

The last.

"Shit." Coop blanched, a wave of unease crashing into him like the first round of a tsunami as he realized that he had permanently removed Scatola, an immortal creature, from the face of existence. He had disabled the last extension. Shutting it down meant there were no other Scatolas to continue the chain of consciousness. He'd killed him.

"Game over man. Game over." Coop fell to his knees beneath the crushing guilt and ramifications of what he'd done. Nausea churned through him, and he bent down, placing his hands flat on the cool concrete floor. He heaved his guts up all over the place. The process went on for a long time.

"Yuck. That has to be the first time in forty years I've puked while sober. It isn't any more fun this way." When he was certain he was done being sick, Coop sat back and tried to breathe.

«Ben? We don't have time for this. We really need to get going. What's wrong?»

"Wrong? I just killed a man. Well, an alien. An alien inside a machine." He shook his head. "I ended a sentient being, Dyrk. I took his life and it really fucking bothers me. That's what is wrong. Okay?"

«But you've killed lots of people. I've watched your movies.»

"Oh, Jesus. Dyrk, those are movies. They aren't real. I was acting. They were acting. When the day ended, they stood up, washed off the special-effects makeup, and we all went and got hammered and fucked strippers. Nobody actually died!" He was screaming by this point.

«Okay, sorry. I'm sorry. But I still don't get it.»

"What about death don't you get? It's really a pretty simple concept."

«If you say so. I've never had to think about it much. That's not what I meant, though. I meant, why are you upset about this *death. He was the bad guy. They all are. The Box aren't cuddly. They're straight villains. You're the hero. You won.»*

"I didn't 'win.' It isn't a game. This isn't a movie either. The rules are different in real life. Nobody wins when people die."

Coop exhaled loudly and closed his eyes.

«You're still a hero.»

"Sure. I'm a hero, Dyrk. I'm also a murderer. Guess which one I'll be discussing with my therapist for the rest of my life."

CHAPTER TWENTY-SEVEN

Cooper remained despondent the entire drive back to the spaceport. He just drove along, absentmindedly stroking Potato's fur with one hand, which the alien creature did not seem to mind one little bit. Dyrk stayed quietly in the background, giving Coop some time to think.

After returning the rental, he tucked Potato inside his jacket and walked through the spaceport to the hotel where Jessica waited with Tycho.

It wasn't a large hotel, but it was opulent. Anything that could have been imported from Earth at great expense had been, from marble flooring to crystal chandeliers and lots of useless but fancy bits of brass in between. It was designed to host the limited number of mining execs, corporate honchos, and transiting dignitaries that passed through Titan, power brokers who had their own arcane reasons for visiting this hellhole and wanted a place that allowed them to make the best of having to be at the spaceport. The kind of people that came in small numbers but with very big wallets.

«This place is swanky,» Dyrk remarked. *«I bet this is the type of place you party at all the time, huh?»*

Coop didn't take the bait. "It's nice of you to try to cheer me up, Dyrk. But I just need time to think."

He inquired at the front desk. Jess must have left his description because a short man in a silly uniform immediately escorted him to a private elevator. It delivered him to the top floor—the fourth—and Coop knocked on the door of Jess' suite. He saw the shadow of feet approach the door and waited while she unlocked and unlatched the portal. He waited some more and heard what he was pretty certain was the sound of furniture being moved away from the door. *That's weird.* Finally, it opened, and Jess waved him inside with a nervous look out into the elevator's foyer.

She began grilling him the moment he shut the door. "Well, how did it go? You have Potato. That's great! But what happened?"

Coop sat down dejectedly in an armchair and stared at Tycho, visible through the open door of an adjacent bedroom, lying on a king-sized bed. "Fine. It went fine, Jess."

"You don't sound fine. Tell me what happened."

"Things went pretty much as planned this morning. We managed to lure the Box to the two locations and deactivate their avatars. It wasn't pretty, but we made a few friends and a lot of money along the way."

"Okay."

"Then we went to the ranch," Coop continued. "The Box left like we planned. But not all of them. We got ambushed in Potato's room, and Pudełko drugged me. It was a pretty close call, but I got lucky. And then, when we were leaving, the last Scatola cut us off in the garage. And I...killed him."

"You mean you deactivated him."

"No, Jess. I didn't 'deactivate' him. I killed him. I shut down the last Scatola. There aren't any of them left."

Jessica laughed.

"You think that's funny? I'm a murderer now. A *murderer*."

"Relax. You can't kill the Box, Mr. Cooper. At least, not from here."

"What's that supposed to mean?"

"There's a reason why we refer to their avatars as 'extensions.' All the Box you've encountered are nothing but adjuncts of their master personas that exist lightyears away on their own home planet. They record and send backups of themselves and the knowledge they've gathered at regular intervals. Sometimes as often as every other day. That's why they have that huge communications suite at the ranch. The only thing you 'killed' is whatever knowledge and experience they'd gained since their last backup. That was probably no more than a few days ago."

"So, I didn't murder him?"

"No, you did not. And if you *had* killed Scatola, from what you've said it would have been self-defense. In the end, he was trying to kill you, wasn't he? But no, somewhere out there in a solar system far, far away is a master Scatola who is just as arrogant and insufferable as the one you know and love."

Dyrk finally spoke up. *«See! We didn't kill anyone. I hope this makes you feel better.»*

"That's a relief!" Coop exclaimed.

"Really?"

"The not being a murderer part. Not the 'master Scatola' part. That part is disturbing."

Coop sat back in his chair to think. He appreciated Jess' ability to sit in silence. He appreciated Tycho's silence less, as it didn't require any effort on her part.

He looked up from his reverie. "Okay, I have a question."

"What is it?"

"Why do they have to do manual updates so frequently?"

Jessica nodded thoughtfully. "I don't know this for a fact, but based on my observations, I suspect it was a condition that allowed specific Box like Scatola, Caja, and Pudełko to have possession of Potato. It ensured their knowledge was shared with the broader Box civilization. Don't forget: Potato has incredible emotional value to their race. The whole time I worked at the ranch, other Box arrived every other month or so as if on a pilgrimage to see it."

"So, more Box will show up expecting to visit Potato."

"Well, yeah."

He felt a growing surge of panic. A moment later, Dyrk gently pushed his consciousness aside and addressed Jessica directly while Coop retreated to process the news that an entire race of jackass aliens might be searching for them soon.

«Hi, doctor, Dyrk here. So, based on what you just told us, if Scatola or the others don't check in with a new backup at the regular time, the other Box are going to get suspicious and send someone to investigate? Depending on how long ago that last backup was, we may not have much time to get what we need and get out of here.»

"Correct. But that information, the timing of the backups, will be in Scatola's log."

«I don't suppose you can access that log?»

Jess grinned and held up her tablet. "Never doubt it."

CHAPTER TWENTY-EIGHT

Jessica sat on a plush divan in the suite's parlor, entered her credentials for Scatola's system, and waited for the data to load.

"Mr. Cooper, why don't you lie down and take a nap? You have to be exhausted."

«I feel fine.»

"Is that Dyrk talking?"

«Well, yes, Dr. Acorns. Coop is resting.»

"Okay, Dyrk. You may feel fine. But your host is human, and while I can't be sure, I suspect he can't really rest unless you do. Humans need rest."

Dyrk paused a moment and then nodded to her. «Coop says you're right. I didn't think about that. Sorry.» Dyrk stood up and crossed to one of the suite's bedrooms to lie down.

Jessica watched until she was certain Dyrk was doing his best to provide Mr. Cooper with some rest and then returned to her data inspection. It didn't take her long to find Scatola's most recent log entry. It was less than a day old.

Author: Scatola-3

Log: 247,820

Subj: human malfeasance

Dr. Acorns and her principal human test subject (Mr. Ben Cooper) demonstrated a complete lack of loyalty and professionalism by violating their contracts. They have absconded with another test subject (Ms. Adrienne Tycho) and one strain of the virus which is resident in Mr. Cooper's personal biology. Efforts to enlist the help of local human authorities have been initiated and all available extensions are involved in the search effort. The virus will be contained or retrieved at any cost.

"Any cost? Great."

Jessica continued her search. She'd always been able to look at Scatola's data. He'd never made a real effort to hide it from her, but she'd never examined it thoroughly. It was part tunnel vision and part integrity on her part that kept her from snooping. Now, as she dug deeper and deeper into his archives, she found a treasure trove of information on the Box and how they functioned as a society.

The doctor was so focused that she hadn't noticed the passage of time. She was surprised when Mr. Cooper appeared behind her and spoke.

"So, what have you found?"

Jessica sighed. "A lot. It's all fascinating, but I'm trying to discern what is actually useful. For a start, I think I understand how the update and communications system works and can extrapolate how it might affect us."

"Okay. Tell me about it." Coop leaned against the side of her sofa, peering at the tablet's display.

"The Box use a null-space transceiver that's a few light seconds away. It resides high above Saturn's position on the ecliptic plane."

"Say what?"

"They use a little satellite to communicate with their home."

"Why didn't you just say that?"

Jessica sighed again. "Scatola's last backup occurred yesterday. That's good news for us. They shouldn't expect another update until tomorrow at the earliest. Given the vagaries of null-space communications, they'll probably wait another day or two before becoming concerned, in case there was a glitch of some sort. If the next backup after *that* doesn't arrive, extensions of Scatola—and likely Caja or Pudełko as well—will arrive to ascertain what has gone wrong."

"So, it's good news and bad news."

"Yes. We have at least a couple of days lead time. But it is almost a certainty that the Box will arrive and begin searching for Potato soon after that."

"Okay. Well, at least we have a head start."

Jessica shook her head. "A head start only helps if you can start running and keep running. I may not have that luxury."

"Why not?"

Jessica sighed heavily and looked at the floor. "While the virus started working on me, it hasn't been curing my disease."

"But it heals everything. How can that be?"

"Actually, that's where I think my initial theory has been wrong. I no longer believe the virus heals you to an *ideal* state. I think it restores you to a more *original* state. Since my disease is part of my DNA, the virus doesn't see it as needing to be fixed. If anything, it's 'improving' the disease by bringing it out of remission. Very soon it will progress to the point where I'm a liability. A short while after that, I'll succumb to a cascade of organ failures and die."

"Fuck that. The virus has to work better than that. You just need to figure it out. You're a genius and I'm good-looking. With that combination we can do anything."

Jessica stared at him, unsure if he was serious or just trying to cheer her up.

"What?"

She shook her head. "Nothing. I am working on an idea. I'll need more equipment to make everything work, and it would be better if we could do it back on Earth. Safer, at least."

"Okay, so what's the problem? We have more than enough cash to buy tickets off Titan."

"The problem, Mr. Cooper, is that the Box will probably show up before the next scheduled ship for Earth. We should definitely be on that ship, we do need to do that, but we'll need to evade the Box if they arrive before we can depart."

The actor smirked. "Dyrk says he still has a stun baton left." At the doctor's confused expression, Coop added, "That's what we used to deactivate all the extensions."

"That sounds like engaging them, not evading."

"Okay, that's a fair point. But… Evade them how?"

"I may know a way, but to make it work we need to go back to the ranch."

Mr. Cooper groaned. "Really?"

Jessica watched as Mr. Cooper's head dropped. She had started to recognize when he and Dyrk were communicating internally.

"I'm being told we should cover our tracks as much as possible. I think it's crazy, but Dyrk is onboard with returning to the ranch."

"We can delete some of the data, which may buy us more time.," Jessica explained. "And there's equipment at the ranch that's not available anywhere else, even on Earth. Diagnostic tools that may allow me to save myself. We really have to do this."

"I hate feeling ganged up on." Mr. Cooper sounded especially petulant.

"You're going to need to get used to that."

"Why?"

"Because I think I can explain Dyrk."

"Come again?"

"I believe Dyrk was able to manifest as a conscious being

because of your bout of null-space syndrome. It left you... susceptible. Think of it as opening a door that allowed a second identity to take up residence in a brain designed for single occupancy."

"So, you're saying Dyrk's a burglar? Like he committed an act of neurologic home invasion? I could have told you that. What does that mean, long term?"

She scrunched up her nose. "I'm not sure. I feel more confident about how he came to be, because my virus has manifested without a Dyrk-like persona. It seems to be spreading throughout my system and doing its work. Heck, my skin hasn't looked this good since before puberty. But I still need more data to figure out what it means."

"Has it worked in Tycho?"

"Yes and no. It's settled in, but it hasn't changed her, even with my attempts to prime it with adrenaline and the audio tracks from its original conditioning. I think we can explain that, now that we have Potato."

"How so?"

"Based on your experiences, and how my own virus didn't begin working until we were in the enclosed environment of a vehicle with Potato, my new hypothesis is that Potato's pheromones act as a catalyst."

"Pheromones? Catalyst? Stick to English, please."

"It means that the scent Potato gives off is a trigger for the virus. One that causes it to mutate and potentiate. This explains why it worked on you, thanks to the adrenaline of the bar fight, but it also explains why the virus leapt to a new level of activity after Potato licked you."

Mr. Cooper frowned and she watched him through another span of internal dialogue.

"Dyrk says that makes sense, and that it also explains Potato's need to be around us. It's a symbiotic thing. So that makes its alien furball spit the magic ingredient."

Jess laughed. "I won't phrase it that way in my journal article. But yeah, that kind of sums it up."

Coop shook his head. "And there's some high-tech, saliva analyzing frizmawhatchit back at the ranch that may hold the key to everything?"

"Pretty much."

He rolled his eyes and sighed. "Fine. I'll call down to the front desk to arrange for a rental to take us back to the ranch. Let's get this over with."

CHAPTER TWENTY-NINE

The fellow with the fancy epaulets personally escorted them to a private garage attached to the hotel, where a vehicle much nicer than Coop's previous rental awaited them for their drive back to the ranch. After a long three-way argument they decided to leave Potato with Tycho to rest rather than risk its presence possibly triggering some security systems at the ranch. Besides, the little alien had experienced more excitement in the previous few days than it had probably known in centuries.

The trip was uneventful, and after reaching and repressurizing the ranch's garage, they exited the vehicle. Coop paused over the crumpled form of the last Scatola extension. Jess came over and patted his back.

"It is only a machine, Mr. Cooper. There was never anything alive about it."

"I know. I know. But it's hard to imagine an identity without a body to identify it by."

"I understand. We'll have lots of time to work out the philosophical stuff later, but right now we have limited time and a lot to accomplish."

Coop knew she was right, so he shook off the feeling of melancholy and followed her into the compound.

Jess led him to her office and shoved a plastic bin into his arms, which she then filled with armloads of notebooks and paper.

"Who uses this much paper?" Coop complained.

Jess paused. "I do. I find it helps me to write things down."

"Can't you type it?"

"It's not the same."

"Is that a scientific answer?"

"Shut up, Mr. Cooper."

"Okay."

Jess continued gathering up her belongings, which became increasingly heavy in Coop's arms. When she finally finished, she put her hands on her hips and looked around her office one last time. "Okay. I think that's everything. Go load it into the car and meet me in the lab. We've got some work to do."

"What's next?"

"Some of this tech is portable and unlike anything available on Earth. I'm going to need it, and from what you said, Scatola was going to blow it all up anyway, so this is fair salvage."

«Speaking of salvage, why don't we put in a call to our good friend Patel?» Dyrk put in.

"What? Why?" Coop demanded.

"Why what, Mr. Cooper?"

"Sorry, Dyrk was suggesting that we call in the, um, pawn-broker who helped, um, dispose of the Box extensions."

Dyrk pointed out, *«He'll probably want any other hardware here that Dr. Acorns can't take with us. Basically, everything that's left in this hab module.»*

"He thinks he might pay for any gear you don't want to take with us."

Jess shrugged. "Couldn't hurt. There's a lot here that's probably valuable that I don't want. You should tell him to bring a big truck."

"Got it."

By the time Patel arrived, Coop had filled the hotel's rental car with all the equipment Jess insisted she needed. They were sitting in the vehicle when a large cargo truck drove into the open garage. Coop closed the outer door and repressurized the garage before stepping out to meet the pawnbroker. Patel had arrived with two large men he introduced as "laborers," and the group followed Jessica on a quick tour of the habitat as she described the hardware available while Patel made notes on a small tablet. After twenty minutes, they returned to the garage.

"You did well, my friend. My buyer will be very pleased."

"Good, then you won't have a problem paying up. Now. I'm feeling generous, so why don't we call it twenty million for everything?"

Behind him, Jess gasped at the amount, but Coop ignored her.

"I appreciate your generosity, Mr. Cooper. But I must address the small matter of the… ahem, condition of the technology. I couldn't help but note that some of it is damaged. This will, of course, affect the price."

"No, it won't."

Patel spread his hands out wide. It made him look even more slimy.

"Surely, Mr. Cooper, you understand that I cannot be expected to pay full price for damaged goods."

"Oh, please. We both know you're not paying anything close to 'full price.' And you're getting more than just hardware. There's all sorts of proprietary data in there too, and it's just fine. Besides, all of this is an extra windfall you weren't expecting, so you're going to come out well ahead. Now, we need to get going. So, pay up."

Patel shook his head, and his bodyguards came over to stand behind him, adopting a menacing posture.

«Come on, I can take these guys. Let me at 'em!»

The doctor bit her lip. "What's going on? I thought you had an arrangement."

"Jess, please. I've got this." Coop sighed. "Mr. Patel, we've dealt with you in good faith. We've produced much more than promised and done so in less time than anticipated. This is your last chance."

Patel looked at the pair of muscled toughs behind him meaningfully. "I am afraid I can't continue to deal with you under these circumstances, Mr. Cooper. In fact, I now feel like I should report you to the authorities. After loading up our truck, of course."

«Like hell, you will.»

"This is your last chance, Patel."

"I think it's time to make you understand the balance of power here, Mr. Cooper. My associates will provide you with a thorough demonstration. It will be painful, but they are professionals and quite quick."

A surge of adrenaline flooded Coop's brain at the threat, and Dyrk jumped into the driver's seat.

«Showtime!»

"I'm sorry?" Patel asked.

«Yeah, you will be.»

Dyrk landed a roundhouse kick to Patel's head, stepped over the little man's body, and drove an elbow into the jaw of one of his henchmen, driving the man backward.

The action hero spun toward the other thug and brought a kick up under the man's jaw. Without bringing his foot down, he snapped another kick to the side of the second man's head, changed feet, and went into a spinning hook kick which caught Patel's man on the opposite side of his face.

The goon lost consciousness before he even hit the floor.

By this time, the first schmuck had recovered and was dancing around his boss' limp body like a prize fighter. It was kind of pathetic.

Jessica backed up against the garage wall and stood watching with a blend of horror and fascination on her face.

Dyrk stalked straight at Patel's thug, who still thought he had a chance. The man threw a quick pair of jabs in his direction, but Dyrk dodged his head out of the way without missing a step. He lunged forward and wrapped his hands around behind his opponent's head. He held tight for just an instant, then drove his forehead into the man's nose with a wet, crackling sound. For good measure, he did it again. The man's body went limp, and Dyrk let go, allowing the flunky to drop to the floor.

Dyrk turned to find Jess staring at him. Her hand covered her mouth and her eyes had gone wide with shock.

"Was that entirely necessary?" she asked.

«Yes. Maybe. Probably not.»

"Then why did you do it?"

«It felt good,» Dyrk explained simply.

"Men are ridiculous."

«I couldn't say. But please remember, you taught me everything I know.»

Jess groaned. "Oh, dear lord. Please stop reminding me."

«Anyway, on the bright side, I suspect he'll be much more ready to bargain when he wakes up naked and hog-tied.»

"Why naked?"

Dyrk tapped his fingers on his chin. «It's just how it's done. It would never occur to me to do otherwise.»

"Okay, Dyrk. I get the psychological value of making him feel vulnerable, but maybe just strip him to his underwear."

Dyrk shrugged. «Whatever. You're the doctor.» He stripped

Patel down to the man's orange leopard-print briefs before securing his wrists and ankles. Then he tied up the pawnbroker's henchmen as well. When he finished, he stepped back and surrendered their shared body to Cooper.

"So now we wait for him to wake up."

"And then what?" asked Jess.

"Then we get the money."

"I don't think you will."

"What? Why would you say that?"

"Because he's a professional scumbag and you're not."

"What's that supposed to mean?"

"I think he knows you'll hurt him, but not actually do him any permanent harm. So if he can stomach some pain, all he has to do is wait us out. And we're the ones who are on the clock, not him."

«She makes a good point,» admitted Dyrk.

"Well, crap. Then how do we get the money?"

Dyrk responded, *«We need a professional of our own. Step into the car and open up the comms. I need to make a call.»*

CHAPTER THIRTY

Less than an hour later, Doug drove an elegant sedan into the garage. He hurried out to open the passenger door for his boss. Al entered the laboratory with Doug following closely on his heels. He looked around and took in the situation. The message from the human, Cooper, had been a surprise and delight to Al.

Given the Box tendency to overcompensate in preparation for even the most unlikely of contingencies, it was a good bet that the habitat was brimming over with proprietary Box technology and data, including a wealth of material that the humans hadn't recognized the value of. Al liked it when business partners over-delivered.

Cooper and the young doctor stood over three other human males they had dragged into the lab. The men were stripped down to their garish underwear and had been secured with tape of some kind. It was the sort of behavior that mortified some humans, though Al had never understood the point. Still, the Clusteran hadn't achieved his level of success by ignoring opportunities. He instructed Doug to record the sad state of Cooper's captives.

Given his own position within the underworld that ran things on Titan, Al recognized Patel and his men as members of the Titan-Tiger crime family. He also knew that they weren't terribly important members. The whole scene was ridiculous, but that too could work to his benefit. He looked at Cooper and smiled.

"Hello, Cooper. You remember my associate, Doug."

"I sure do." The actor turned to Dr. Acorns. "Jess this is Al, and the guy with him is—"

"Oh, I know Doug." She crossed her arms.

Al briefly wondered what that was about but decided to let it slide for the moment. He made a mental note to debrief Doug at a later date. Other tasks took priority. "Doug, go check out the facility. See what the most valuable items are. We can't guarantee we'll get multiple trips, so we need to get the best stuff now."

"Will do." Doug left the lab and proceeded down the corridor.

Al returned his attention to Cooper and the hog-tied lowlifes at his feet. "For an actor known for his charm, you seem to make a lot of people angry."

Cooper grinned back at him. "When it comes to scumbags like Mr. Patel here, I'm of two minds."

Al felt like he missed an inside joke but didn't let it stop him. "Am I here for these men? That wasn't part of our earlier conversation."

"Sort of. You see, Mr. Patel here has reneged on his agreement with us. In fact, he tried to muscle us out of millions of dollars worth of Box tech. Needless to say, his negation of our deal opens up an opportunity to strike a new agreement."

The alien looked around at the medical equipment. "Is the rest of the building stocked like this?"

Jessica jumped in. "Actually, better. I've removed several items from here for my own use. There are three more laboratories and an infirmary, all fully stocked. Plus the communications suite and the security equipment."

Al let out a slow breath. "Well, that presents quite the opportunity. What was your deal with Mr. Patel?"

Coop filled him in on the original arrangement and his generous offer of asking only twenty million.

Toward the end of their discussion, Patel groaned and opened his eyes. Al watched as the bound man glared at Cooper and threatened him.

"I'm going to kill you."

Coop looked down. "How?"

Patel blinked and pulled at his bonds. "Why am I tied up?"

Coop laughed. "Well, you tried to rob us and have me beaten to a pulp. Then, the first thing you did upon waking up was to threaten to kill me. It seemed like the way to go."

Patel nodded. "That seems reasonable. But, my friend, please realize, it was just business. Don't take it personally."

Coop nodded and pointed toward Al. "I'm glad to hear you say that, Patel. Please don't take this personally. It's just business."

The bound human followed Coop's finger and saw Al for the first time. Patel gulped audibly.

Al stepped forward. "Cooper, I have a proposal that I believe will resolve all of your concerns."

"I'm listening."

With the nonchalance of a man who'd already eaten looking through a menu, Al laid out his plan. "I am familiar with the human expression about possession and its accounting for ninety percent of legal authority. Based on this and the current absence of any Box on Titan, I will stipulate that you are the owner of everything here."

"I think I like where this is headed. Go on."

"You sell me Mr. Patel. You sell me all the technology remaining in the ranch. In return, I will pay you double what you had asked of Mr. Patel for all of it. Plus, I will complete your travel arrangements and pay off your hotel bill. We'll be even, and you'll have considerably more money than you have now. How does that sound?"

The actor grinned, until Dr. Acorn leaned in close and argued,

"Mr. Cooper, we can't sell him a human being! That is unacceptable."

Coop sighed. "What do you mean when you say 'sell' you Patel?"

The alien nodded. "I understand your hesitance. I am not buying him physically. I simply desire for you to authorize me to negotiate a new arrangement with him. In return, I will provide you everything I have promised."

Coop looked at Jessica. She seemed mollified.

"Okay, Al. Go for it."

The alien turned his dark eyes to Patel. "You heard? Let me be clear, the word 'negotiation' is a fiction. These are the terms: You will transfer to this man's account the full payment I have described," he gestured toward Coop. "Do not offer any complaints. You will be allowed to keep the extensions you currently possess, and we both know your profits from them will more than cover this new expense. As for the rest of the tech here, it is mine. Is that clear?"

Patel looked like he wanted to argue. Coop could almost hear the hamster wheel turning in the man's head as he searched desperately for a way out of his predicament.

Al grew impatient. "You can refuse, of course. But if you do, I will call in your family's debts. Today. And I will inform your uncle that you are responsible for forcing my hand."

Patel's eyes got very wide. "Where do I sign?"

Al smiled and produced a tablet. "Right here, Mr. Patel. Right here."

A short time later, a very dejected-looking Patel had departed the compound with his henchmen in the vehicle Al and Doug had come in, leaving behind their empty truck. Before driving off, he had transferred an astonishing sum of money to the account Dyrk had set up earlier.

Doug was still making his rounds through the compound, and Al wasted no more time getting down to the next piece of business. The alien produced a folder from his jacket. "As promised, here are your new identification documents. I have also included your travel itinerary, which contains arrangements for your friend's medical needs and the authorizations for importing a rare alien creature."

Inside Coop's head, Dyrk asked, «*So we get everything we asked for, all of our other expenses covered, and an additional forty million for the tech here in the habitat? You think maybe we settled too cheaply?*»

Dyrk?

«*Yeah, Coop?*»

Shut up.

Coop accepted the documents. "Thank you, Al. It has been a pleasure doing business with you."

The alien looked around the laboratory hungrily. "The pleasure is all mine, Mr.…Fuentes."

Coop looked down at the identification documents. "Fuentes?"

Al laughed.

EPILOGUE

Ensconced in the luxury presidential suite courtesy of Al's generosity, Coop had his feet up on the table. One hand rested inside the pocket of his very fluffy bathrobe, and the other held a cup of steaming coffee.

The suite was beautiful. The furniture was posh. The décor was a tasteful blend of blue and gray shades with bright orange accents punctuating the tranquil space. Soft decorative pillows dotted the luxurious landscape, and a bar full of consumable delights sat fully stocked nearby. It resembled the type of place Coop felt he deserved. This was the way an acclaimed movie actor should be treated. He let out a satisfied sigh as he took a bite of his croissant and raised his coffee mug to his nose.

"God, this coffee smells good."

"I'm glad it makes you happy." Jess walked around the blue chaise lounge where they had moved Tycho. The doctor paused every so often to stare at the monitors she had liberated from the Box ranch and muttered to herself. She even paused to point some kind of sensor in his direction before frowning in concentration. Coop didn't mind.

"This is a lot more like it. No more experiments. No more

stupid aliens. Well, except for Potato." He reached down and affectionately patted the furball resting under his legs.

Jess walked toward Coop with a syringe in one gloved hand. "Don't get too comfortable, Mr. Cooper. I need more blood and we still need to get back to Earth. I'll feel a lot safer once we're there."

"I know. I'm just enjoying the moment. I want to get home too." Coop rolled his sleeve up so Jess could continue her analysis of the virus and its effects on his system.

«I don't know why she keeps taking blood. I feel fine.» Dyrk objected.

"Dyrk says he feels fine and you can stop taking blood."

The doctor didn't even look up. "Tell Dyrk thank you, but I'll be the judge of what is fine."

"Jess says…"

«I heard her. I heard her. I was just trying to help.»

As if she heard him, Jess continued. "Tell Dyrk if he wants to help, he can double check that our fake IDs are all in order and that our digital footprints have been scrubbed adequately. I don't exactly trust your friend Al."

«Done and done, sweetheart.»

Coop cringed. Even he knew not to relay that message verbatim. He'd been rubbing off on Dyrk more than was probably good. "He says it's taken care of."

Jess huffed, started to place a bandage on Coop's arm, but the skin had already healed.

As she walked away, Potato hopped up to see what was going on. It had been a lot more active and had even developed a bit of a personality. Sure, it was simple and goofy, but it was really adorable.

"Potato has gotten really clingy."

«We're related, and it senses the connection,» Dyrk explained again. Coop hugged the alien fuzzball and glanced at Jess as she tapped away on her tablet.

"What are you working on?"

"Hmmm?"

"I asked what you are working on."

Jess stopped typing. "Sorry. I'm just running with an idea. Maybe a really good idea. But..."

"What?"

"I need to ask Dyrk a few questions, and it would be easier if I could ask them directly. Nuance matters. But asking you to switch places with him seems...rude."

Coop sighed. "Don't sweat it. It's becoming really easy for us to swap, and as much as I hate to say it, I'm getting used to it. It's still weird, but it doesn't freak me out anymore. Okay, Dyrk. You're up."

Coop slid his consciousness aside as Dyrk came to the fore.

«Hi, Dr. Acorns. How can I help?» Dyrk asked.

"Coop told me about how you changed his eyes at the ranch. Can you explain the process to me, please?"

«Sure. It isn't really that complicated. I just rearranged his DNA to create new eyes from the molecular level on up. Pretty simple.»

"You call that 'simple'?"

«Oh yeah, absolutely. It's just DNA. For me, it's like playing with Legos.»

Jess shook her head slowly. "DNA is like Legos? Okay. Sure. And this is because you control the virus. Right?"

«Correct. Kind of. Maybe.»

"It's a simple question, Dyrk, and I need a straight answer. Either you can or you can't. Which is it?"

«It's not so simple, doctor. The virus and I are linked, but it's not as though I'm in charge of it. We're distinct. I'm me, and I'm not it. It responds to me, sure, but it's... Well, I guess 'instinctive' is as good a word as any for how it works.»

Jess frowned at the explanation. "That doesn't make any sense. You're a manufactured persona. You don't have instincts."

Dyrk shrugged as eloquently as anything Coop had done on screen. «I don't know how else to explain it. I'm working with the concepts and vocabulary from the films that made me.»

"Of course, that explains it!"

Coop chimed in internally, *Explains what?*

«Ben would like to know what that explains. Me too.»

"It's all about perspective. You're like my tablet." She held up the device.«Your tablet?» "It lets me monitor readings, access networks, perform experiments. It has multiple applications that allow me to do many different things, but none of those apps are the motivating force behind any of what they do. It's just a tool, an interface."

«And how does that relate to me?»

I think she just called you a tool, Coop suggested.

"The same seems to be true of the virus. Like my tablet, it's a tool. But you need to know how to use it. Failing that, you need a smarter interface. I have the virus in me. It's trying to work, but it doesn't have the needed direction."

«Because you lack the right interface?»

"I think so. All I've managed is to kick it into a default mode, which leaves me worse off than when I started. But Mr. Cooper doesn't have that problem, because he has you."

«So… What? I'm an interface between Ben and the virus?»

"That, and maybe much more. You said yourself that your connection to the virus occurs at an instinctual level. Do you think you could control it when it isn't in Mr. Cooper's body?"

Dyrk considered this for a moment. «I don't see why not. It's not something I'm consciously doing. Like when you tell your arm to reach out and catch something thrown at you. It just happens.»

Jess stood and grabbed two vials of blood from the table next to Tycho. She presented them to Dyrk. "Can you tell the difference between these two blood samples? Both contain the virus?"

Dyrk wrinkled his brow in concentration. He frowned. «No… they're just glass tubes to me.»

Pop the seals, Coop instructed Dyrk.

«*What?*»

Open the vials and sniff them. Potato is all about smells, right?

Before the doctor could stop him, Dyrk thumbed the stoppers off each tube.

"What are you doing?"

«Ben had an idea. Oh, yeah. They're completely different.» He raised the vial in his left hand. «This is yours. That's obvious now. And this other one belongs to Tycho.»

Jess took a deep breath. "You're responding to the different versions of the virus in each?"

«I guess.»

"Can you change one sample to match the other?"

Dyrk closed his eyes. He pursed his lips and blew lightly across the opening of each vial. A few minutes passed before he opened his eyes and stared back at Jess. «Done.»

Jess snatched the samples back and ran them over to a machine that rested on a marble-topped buffet, another piece of equipment liberated from the Box ranch. She inserted the vials and stared at her tablet as the results populated.

"You did it. It's possible."

«What's possible?»

"That maybe I don't have to die. Earlier, I had the idea that if I added Tycho's version of the virus to my body, it could beat back the version that's reactivated my disease and is keeping me healthy even as it marches me toward a massive organ failure cascade. But it won't work. The version I started with is already too firmly lodged in me. Her version is too little too late."

«I'm very sorry to hear that, doctor.»

"No, you don't understand. The idea is sound. But it's like I was saying about the tablet before. The virus on its own doesn't have the guidance to get the job done. And the job is very straightforward. We just have to change my cells and alter my genetics so I don't have the disease."

«Oh. That would be good.»

Jess nodded. She even smiled a little. "Yes, Dyrk. It would be very good."

«And you want me to be the interface to make that happen? What do you need me to do?»

"It's the same idea as you used to change Mr. Cooper's eyes at the cellular level. You're going to instruct my virus to change me, head to toe, every single cell. You can do that, right?"

«Yes, I think so. It's the same thing as altering a few cells, just a difference in scale. But…your virus will just change you back.»

"Not if the conversion is into someone who already has the virus busily maintaining their own genetic blueprint."

Coop pushed his way through to regain control of his body. "Jess, what are you talking about? There's no such person."

"There is," insisted Dr. Jessica Acorns. She glanced to the chaise lounge where the comatose body of the third recipient of her experiment laid. "I want you to change me into a clone of Tycho!"

AUTHORS' NOTE

WRITTEN AUGUST 6, 2022

We are not a natural fit as co-authors. There's more than a few years difference in our ages, our lives have taken very different paths, and our personal tastes diverge greatly. For instance, while we both enjoy the breadth of speculative fiction, our passions are not the same.

Lawrence grew up on a steady diet of Science Fiction's so-called Golden Age and segued from the "Rockets and Rivets" into the "New Wave" with its growing emphasis on social sciences. As a precocious reader, he devoured all of Heinlein and Burroughs and slipped into his teenage years switching over to Zelazny, Le Guin, and Delany. There was still plenty of the classic "sense o' wonder," but the perspective had shifted to a more humanistic focus.

In the midst of this, *Star Trek* came along, and that was it. He was hooked. Those heady progressive days of the original five year mission have remained a big part of his professional life leading him to pursue an education as a research psychologist and set him up to be a college professor. They can probably also be blamed for his work over the past thirty years promoting the Klingon language around the world. **majQa'**.

Brian loved everything to do with fantasy from an early age. As a young child he was obsessed with knights and castles and drew some really-freaking-awesome stick figure archers with flaming arrows. Those battles were epic.

But around the 5th grade, Brian came across a book called *Dragons of Autumn Twilight* by Weis and Hickman. He was instantly hooked on the world of Krynn with its tri-colored mages, kender, and chromatically segregated dragons. He loved it and tore through dozens of books set in this world. Then he discovered R.A. Salvatore and his protagonist, Drizzt Do'Urden. Many dog-eared pages ensued and less homework was completed on time thanks to these amazing stories.

Quite naturally, these books led Brian to Dungeons and Dragons which led down the road to Shadowrun and Cyberpunk. And later in life authors like Jim Butcher and, Naomi Novik, and J.K. Rowling accompanied him on deployments to Iraq and Afghanistan and continued to fuel his interest in all things fantastic.

Now, if you've read our books with LMBPN, you know they don't much resemble any of these things that helped define Brian. Nor do they fit neatly with Lawrence's literary passions. But they do represent a light version of our shared interests. Our books aren't as epic as either of us might choose. They aren't as dark as Brian might write and they aren't as quirky as Lawrence tends to produce on his own. But we hope they are fun for you to read. They have certainly been fun for us to write, and our partnership in bringing you these stories has sustained both of us at very difficult times in our lives. It is our hope that others else may find a small bit of joy from them when they need it.

ACKNOWLEDGMENTS

If you're the sort of person who reads book's Acknowledgment section (and hey,you're here now, right?) then you know that a book is never the product of just the authors listed on the cover. This is especially true when that book gets updated and republished.

Once again, we want to express our appreciation to the 20Books community, the family of indie authors that ranges from enthusiastic beginners to famous superstars, bound together by mutual support, motivation, and inspiration. We share our struggles and our victories, our strategies and tactics, to the betterment of all, because that's what family is supposed to do.

This book, the one that preceded it and the one that comes after, are only possible because the folks at LMBPN saw in them what we saw, and gave them new life. I refer, of course, to Michael, Judith, Robin, Kelly, Steve, and the many others on the LMBPN who do all the jobs so essential to publishing. Particular thanks to our fabulous LMBPN beta-readers for the series, Rachel Beckford, Larry Omans, Kelly O'Donnell, John Ashmore, Mary Morris, and editors Lynne Stiegler and Jacqui Scherrer, who make our words that much more coherent for you, the reader.

Jake Clark provided the incredible artwork that graces our covers and lets you know at a glance just what kind of a ride awaits as soon as you turn the page.

Finally, as is our way, we need to acknowledge and thank the women in our lives, brave souls that they are for putting up with us. It is not an easy thing to live with authors, let alone do so with grace and style. They give us so much better than we deserve. It must surely be love.

ABOUT BRIAN THORNE

Brian Thorne is a former Marine and intelligence officer. These days, he works in cybersecurity when he's not playing chauffeur to his son or training his new rescue dog. If those activities allow him spare time, he tries to write.

A recent transplant to Texas, Thorne has undertaken a noble quest to find the perfect brisket and share news of it with the world. He views it as his crowning contribution to humanity.

To follow Brian on his writing adventure, keep up to date on his brisket quest, and receive a free short story, you can join his newsletter at http://bit.ly/ThorneNews. Your email address will not be sold, rented, or in any other way disseminated.

ABOUT LAWRENCE M. SCHOEN

Lawrence M. Schoen holds a Ph.D. in cognitive psychology and psycholinguistics. He spent ten years as a college professor, doing research in the areas of human memory and language. This was followed by seventeen years as the director of research for a medical center in Philadelphia that provided mental health and addiction services.

He's also the founder of the Klingon Language Institute, and since 1992, he has championed the exploration and use of this constructed tongue throughout the world. In addition, he occasionally works as a hypnotherapist specializing in authors' issues. He is also a cancer survivor.

In 2007, he was a finalist for the Astounding Award for Best New Writer. He received a Hugo Award nomination for Best Short Story in 2010 and Nebula Award nominations for Best Novella in 2013, 2014, 2015, and 2018, for Best Novelette in 2019, and for Best Novel in 2016.

Some of his most popular writing deals with the ongoing humorous adventures of a spacefaring stage hypnotist named the Amazing Conroy and his companion animal Reggie, an alien buffalito that can eat anything and farts oxygen.

His *Barsk* series represents his serious work and uses anthropomorphic SF to explore ideas of prophecy, intolerance, political betrayal, speaking to the dead, predestination, and free will. It's also earned him the Cóyotl Award for Best Novel of 2015 and again in 2018.

Lawrence lives near Philadelphia with his wife Valerie, who is neither a psychologist nor a Klingon speaker.

If you would like updates on Lawrence's new releases, appearances, or special offers, please consider joining his mailing list. Your email address will not be sold, rented, or in any other way disseminated. Simply use this link to sign up: http://bit.ly/LMS-join

ALSO BY LAWRENCE M. SCHOEN

Barsk

Barsk: The Elephants' Graveyard

(2015 Nebula Award Finalist, 2015 Winner Cóyotl Award)

The Moons of Barsk

(2018 Winner Cóyotl Award)

Excerpts of Jorl ben Tral

Soup of the Moment

Pizlo's Limits

SERIES IN THE "CONROYVERSE"

Conroyverse: A Sampler

("Buffalo Dogs," *Buffalito Destiny, Ace of Corpses,* and *Slice of Entropy*)

The Amazing Conroy

Buffalito Bundle

(includes "Yesterday's Taste," 2011 WSFA Small Press Award Finalist)

Barry's Tale

(2012 Nebula Award Finalist)

Calendrical Regression

(2014 Nebula Award Finalist)

Barry's Deal

(2017 Nebula Award Finalist)

Buffalito Destiny

Trial of the Century

(2013 Nebula Award Finalist)

Buffalito Contingency

Command Performance

(The Amazing Conroy Omnibus Edition)

Freelance Courier

Ace of Corpses

Ace of Saints

Ace of Thralls

Ace of Agency

(Freelance Courier Books 1 – 3)

Pizza In Space

Slice of Entropy

Slice of Chaos

Humaniversity (with Catherine M. Petrini)

Dorms of Asgard

Pirates of Sol

Pirates of Marz

Seeds of War (with Jonathan Brazee)

Invasion

Scorched Earth

Bitter Harvest

Seeds of War Trilogy

Adrenaline Rush (with Brian Thorne)

Fight or Flight

Alien Thrill Seeker

Anger Management

The Demon Codex (with Brian Thorne)

Soul Bottles

At the Speed of Yeti

Undead Alternatives

Collections

Creature Academy: Cautionary Poems of Public Education

Sweet Potato Pie and other stories

The Rule of Three and other stories

Openings without Closure

Transcendent Boston and other stories

Non-Fiction

Eating Authors: One Hundred Writers' Most Memorable Meals

Author Website:

http://www.lawrencemschoen.com/books/

OTHER BOOKS FROM LMBPN PUBLISHING

Sign up for the LMBPN email list to be notified of new releases and special deals!

https://lmbpn.com/email/

For a complete list of books by LMBPN please visit:

https://lmbpn.com/books-by-lmbpn-publishing/

www.ingramcontent.com/pod-product-compliance
Lightning Source LLC
LaVergne TN
LVHW041931070526
838199LV00051BA/2772
* 9 7 9 8 8 8 5 4 1 7 4 5 7 *